DEATH TRADER

DEATH TRADER

A PROJECT MOLKA NOVEL

Fredrick. L. Stafford

Acknowledgement

My heartfelt thanks to a very special person and friend Michelle Kirk. This book and the PROJECT MOLKA Series would not have come to life without her. She served as both a model and creative consultant during the development of the lead character. Her insights, enthusiasm, and words of encouragement were invaluable to me. I will be ever grateful for her inspiration, friendship, and unwavering support.

 CHAPTER ONE

"If you live through this you'll never be the same," the skinny bearded man said to the beautiful young woman. "And I won't lie. It's going to be more horrible than you can imagine. But making us mad at you will only make it worse. So, you better answer my question."

The beautiful young woman remained silent and memorized the name badge clipped on his sweat stained work shirt: Jaron.

"I'm already mad at her," the stocky bearded man said. "But she's about to make me enraged. And trust me, bitch, you don't want that. Answer his question."

She remained silent and memorized the name badge clipped on his sweat and food stained work shirt: Dov.

"Better listen to him," Jaron said. "The last girl who made him enraged didn't want to answer my question either. Then he made sure she can't answer questions anymore."

Dov's beard parted and exposed an obscene grin. "That's right. And that slut wasn't really my type. You, I can't wait to put my hands on. Answer his question. Now."

She remained silent.

Jaron pointed a grimy bone he used for a finger at her. "I'll ask you one last time. Are you ready to have some fun with us tonight, baby?"

Being their intended rape victim in the dark deserted parking lot didn't surprise her. She had predicted it. She had come to accept it. She even looked forward to it.

The day her assault occurred began as normal for the beautiful young woman. She left her loft apartment in Tel Aviv's Azorei Hen neighborhood before dawn and went to the gym. No one there. Good. No one to stare at her tall lean muscular body. No one to ask questions about her intense routine. No one to make lame propositions.

After working out, she drove to her office in an isolated warehouse district. Her solo veterinary practice had a small, but loyal client base. People appreciated her compassion and professionalism. She treated every pet as her own. And when she left on one of her extended business trips, she always made sure to recommend an alternate clinic for their care.

She put on a white lab coat and pulled her straight dark hair into a ponytail. A native Israeli tan hid her pale skin, but the prominent cheek bones, sharp chin, and large oval shaped blue eyes behind her black-framed glasses revealed old-world Eastern European heritage.

"Good morning, Mrs. Friedman." She greeted an elderly lady in her office waiting area. "I see you've brought Gavi again."

Mrs. Friedman held a pet carrier containing a black and tan Pekingese. She wept. "Please help my precious little Gavi, doctor."

"Mrs. Friedman, as I've told you, I'm not trained to perform such a specialized surgery. Have you taken him to Doctor Cohen as I recommended?"

"Doctor Cohen's fee is beyond my means to pay. I am on a very fixed income. He suggested euthanizing my poor Gavi. Can you please help us?"

"I'm sorry to hear this, Mrs. Friedman. However, you must also consider that Gavi is fourteen years old and near the end of his natural lifespan. Even if he receives the surgery, he's unlikely to live much longer."

Through fresh tears, Mrs. Friedman said, "My husband has been gone over ten years. Now I will lose my Gavi and be all alone in this world. But you are still young; you do not yet understand what it is like to lose the ones you love."

After Mrs. Friedman left, the beautiful young woman contacted Doctor Cohen and arranged to pay for precious little Gavi's lifesaving surgery herself. She could go another year without a vacation.

The day her assault occurred continued as usual. New puppy and kitten visits, sick animals, vaccinations, examining lumps and bumps, and a suture removal.

She ate lunch, as always, at her desk.

Her day ended with a few more appointments and meticulous paperwork. Time to leave. A check out the window confirmed two men leaning against the lone car in the dark deserted parking lot. The car was hers. The men were Jaron and Dov.

She had first encountered them three weeks before, unloading trucks at a warehouse across the street from her office. Every morning when she arrived, they stopped working and shouted vulgar comments and questions at her. She ignored them, but her silence only caused their comments and questions to increase in vulgarity. Each day they became more aggressive. Their aggression converted to anger. She thought it might end badly. And a week before her assault occurred when she found a roadkill cat carcass on her office doorstep with a note saying, "You're next, pussy cat," she knew it would end badly.

She opened her shoulder bag and rechecked the contents. Satisfied, she shouldered it, switched off the lights, locked the door behind her, and stepped into a cool and desolate night. Jaron and Dov still leaned against her car. She approached them. Their combined body odor offered her a hostile greeting. She stopped a few feet away. They slithered off the car and spewed her with their most vulgar comments and questions yet.

She remained silent. Until…

Jaron pointed a grimy bone he used for a finger at her. "I'll ask you one last time. Are you ready to have some fun with us tonight, baby?"

The beautiful young woman removed her glasses, put them in her bag, placed her bag on the pavement, smiled, and said, "I promise to give you my answer, but first may I ask each of you a question?"

Jaron leered. "That's it, baby. Try to talk your way out. Beg us. Makes it better for me when they beg. But yes, you may. Go ahead."

She addressed Jaron. "How are you going to ask your question to the next girl with your jaw wired shut for the next six weeks or so?"

Jaron stopped leering.

She addressed Dov. "And will you want to put your hands on anyone else, or even yourself, after they've been permanently crippled?"

"You've got a brave mouth, baby," Jaron said. "It's going to be a pleasure choking it shut."

Dov said, "But first I'm going to pay her back for every smart-ass slut word she just said, one scream at a time."

"What do you have to say about that, baby?" Jaron said.

Her smile faded. "Nothing is decided until it's decided."

"She's only stalling," Dov said. "No more questions. No more answers. Let's take the bitch behind the building and do this."

"Ok, let's." Jaron took a single step toward her.

She sprung on him, applied a neck clinch, pulled his head down, and rammed her knee into his jaw.

It shattered.

He dropped.

Dov grabbed for her with instinctive shock.

She clamped a wristlock on his right wrist and butchered it.

He screamed, fell to his knees, and grabbed for her with his left hand.

Another wristlock butchered his left wrist.

He screamed again, fell to his face, and kept screaming.

Jaron got up. He shouldn't have.

Her whisper short of a deathblow hook kick to his temple put him straight back down.

She followed with a merciless axe kick to Dov's head as a scream silencer.

Both men laid crumpled and semi-conscious. She grasped Jaron under his arms, dragged him to her car, and propped him against the door in a sitting position. With a bit more effort, she placed Dov next to him.

She reached into her bag and removed leather tactical gloves and latex medical gloves. She put the leather gloves on her hands and the latex gloves over the leather. Next, she straightened the bearded heads, assumed a fighting stance, and violated their faces with punches. Each man gave up a broken nose. She paused, changed her stance, and pumped in even harder blows. Their eyes disappeared under contusions.

Her empowerment peaked. Both men slumped onto their sides unconscious. She stopped the trauma. She got what she wanted. She was satiated. Spent. Done.

But not quite.

She debased them with a few final rib-fracturing kicks—for disrespecting the poor cat.

The beautiful young woman stood over the broken human debris piles and recomposed herself. Then she removed the blood-stained latex gloves, tossed one on each man, removed the leather gloves, dropped them in her bag, picked the bag off the pavement, took out her glasses, put them on, smiled, and said, "Now, as promised, I'll answer your question. Yes, I was ready to have some fun with you both tonight. And I certainly did. Thank you, this was just what I needed."

An hour after she left them to fate, a passerby called the police. The police called an ambulance. The stunned veteran paramedics asked what happened to the car the men crashed in.

And when they regained consciousness in the hospital—Jaron with his jaw wired shut for the next six weeks and Dov with his permanently crippled hands in casts—they didn't tell the police they were put there by a beautiful young woman they had intended to assault.

It wouldn't have mattered anyway.

They never really knew what hit them

They never really knew who hit them.

They never really knew the beautiful young woman.

They never really knew Molka.

 CHAPTER TWO

BOOM. BOOM. BOOM.

"Damn! That was close!"

BOOM. BOOM. BOOM.

"That was closer! There's a 23-millimeter on that rooftop! Get us out of here, Lieutenant!"

BOOM. BOOM. BOOM.

"We're hit! Use the fire extinguisher!"

BOOM. BOOM. BOOM.

"Hydraulics failure. We're going down. Let's try for a running landing in that field, Ilan. Everyone put your belts on! Brace for impact!"

Molka awoke braced for impact—in her bed. The nightmare ended, but the BOOMING continued. Someone knocked on her front door. It was still dark; 5:02 AM showed on the nightstand clock. She gripped the Beretta 96A1 pistol beside it. No, the one to kill her wouldn't knock. It could only be him.

She barefooted downstairs in a long white tee over light blue panties. The peephole confirmed her assumption. She unlocked and opened the door to a man.

"Time for us to talk again," the man said.

"Yes, it is. Because I asked you never to come here, Azzur."

Azzur entered uninvited. He exhibited exceptional fitness for a man in his early fifties, complemented by a clear dark complexion and neatly groomed gray-specked black hair. He wore a fashionable brown leather jacket and carried a matching leather satchel. Many women found him attractive, Molka not included.

Molka shut the door behind him. "This is my home. My private life. I didn't agree to invasions of either."

"You agreed to serve me," Azzur said.

"I agreed to serve my country."

"As far as it pertains to you, I am your country now."

Molka entered her pristine kitchen and flipped on the light. On the counter, a calico she sometimes let spend the night blinked twice and departed. When she opened the refrigerator and bent to retrieve a bottled water she sensed Azzur contemplating her nakedness under the thin t-shirt.

"I would offer to make you coffee," Molka said. "But you might stay longer than absolutely necessary. This couldn't be done in my office during a decent business hour?"

Azzur sat at the kitchen table and took out and lit a cigarette.

"No, really; it's fine," Molka said. "Go ahead and smoke in my house. I don't mind." She threw open the window over the sink, retrieved a saucer from a cupboard, and tossed it on the table for ashtray duty.

Azzur opened his satchel, removed a tablet, and placed it on the table.

Molka sat opposite him. "Typical. They gave you an awesome new briefing tablet, but I still can't get reimbursed for my range ammo."

"You leave for the United States in twenty-four hours," Azzur said. "Florida." He opened a folder on the tablet's desktop and a man's unflattering headshot photo appeared.

Molka stuck her tongue out. "Ugh. Who's the pretty boy?"

"That fat snake is Mr. Gaszi Sago. We will discuss him in a moment."

"Can't wait. Ok, I'm going to Florida. What's my legend?"

"Same as last time: the veterinarian exchange program. You have been accepted to serve as a guest physician at the Kind Kare Animal Hospital in the city of Cinnamon Cove, an exclusive beach community north of Miami. The hospital was impressed by your background. More accurately your origins. The area is largely populated by our kinfolk. Therefore, you will fit in unobtrusively."

"Just another nice girl from the neighborhood?"

"Yes. And I believe the improvement in your English gained by your time with the American Captain will serve you well."

Molka paused her water sip. "If there's something you *don't* know about me yet, please tell me. I'd like to be buried with at least one secret."

Azzur blew smoke and went on, "Mr. Sago is leasing an oceanside mansion near the animal hospital. He has two dogs he always travels with and is obsessed with their wellbeing. He oddly refers to them as his 'children.' Day after tomorrow, he has an appointment to bring his dogs to this hospital for a routine checkup. This is how you will make contact."

"Good intel. The associates have been busy."

Azzur swiped the tablet to a new page showing several more photos. "You will be provided with this leased car—waiting for you at the airport—and this apartment located near the hospital. Fully furnished."

"Looks nice. Fully furnished including my weapons, of course."

"No weapons should be necessary for this task."

"Maybe not, but that part of our agreement is definitely non-negotiable. Remember?"

Azzur grudged her a nod. "Your preferred weapons and accessories will be in the apartment. However, we did not have time to obtain a concealed weapons license for you. Therefore, I would not recommend getting frisked by any local authorities."

"I wouldn't recommend that either."

"The apartment also contains a regular cell phone for general use and an encrypted cell phone for secure communications. Also, twenty-five thousand US dollars in cash."

Molka bounced in her chair. "Oooo. I know a girl who's going shopping."

"The cash is for task related expenses only. Besides, I already arranged for you to have a complete wardrobe waiting there."

"A complete wardrobe, you say? Well, I hope you didn't buy me any capri pants. I hear those are so *two years ago* in Miami."

Molka smiled. Azzur did not.

"What's my exit tale?" Molka said.

"Your sweet Aunt Zillah will become gravely ill, and you must come home immediately to care for her."

"Do I have a sweet Aunt Zillah?"

Azzur pointed to his face. "You are looking at her."

"Ew, auntie, you need a shave."

Molka smiled again.

"I am happy you are in such good humor, Molka. Especially considering the results of your first task."

Molka's smile faded. "My immigration status?"

"Everything legal. All in your real name."

"Now tell me the good part." Molka swiped the tablet back to the man's photo. "Who is he, and why am I making contact with him?"

"He is an enemy of the State."

"Can you be a little vaguer, please?"

Azzur flicked ash on the saucer. "As your Project Manager I hoped by your second task that these types of irrelevant questions would be reduced to a minimum."

"And as your project I hoped by my second task to have a different Project Manager. Neither one of us got our wish."

Azzur smiled. "Very well. With you projects we make special allowances, due to your neophyte status."

"Hey, we neophytes are people too."

"Mr. Sago is a Hungarian national. Fifty-seven years old. He is a successful commodities trader of great renown. Married but never seen with his wife. Exceedingly wealthy, educated, cultured, well-traveled, fluent in English, Russian, French, and German, a womanizer, arrogant, and in the finest tradition of Hungarian businessmen, a ruthless conman with many dubious connections."

Molka shrugged. "That could describe a lot of businessmen anywhere. What did he do to us?"

"He assisted the Traitors. More specifically, he acted as their middleman. He was the one who sold the Traitors information to our enemies. He will be called into account for this."

10

"Then you chose the wrong girl." Molka picked up the briefing tablet, pressed it into Azzur's chest, and held it there. "I told you I won't be an assassin for you. Or a murderer."

Azzur smiled again. "Molka, you must put more practice into your righteous indignation act. In any case, your military service record betrays you. Your Unit assassinated people. Many, many people. Including some who were not supposed to be assassinated. And by the law, that is murder."

"We did our best. We made some mistakes. Those regrets continue."

"You may fear no further regrets here." Azzur took the tablet from her hands and laid it back on the table. "Mr. Sago is to be delivered to us undamaged. The Counsel have many questions for him. Then perhaps, other uses. He will likely be our guest for a very long time."

"Can't we just ask the US authorities to pick him up and hold him for us?"

"Significant American friends of ours do not wish Mr. Sago to be detained. To the contrary, they wish for him to conclude his business and leave United States soil alive and coherent. On this point they are quite adamant."

"Why would these significant American friends of ours care about him leaving alive and coherent?"

"For their plausible deniability reasons, I would surmise. Nevertheless, nothing for you to concern yourself with."

"Yes, sir." Molka saluted Azzur with the wrong hand. "Anyway, Sago brings his dogs to this animal hospital for a routine checkup. What am I supposed to do? Walk up and politely ask him to join me on a nice seventeen-hour transatlantic flight? Oh, and by the way Gaszi sweetie, when we land, the torturers would like to have a long talk with you."

"We prefer to call them the auditors."

"Agony by any other name, is still agony."

"Mr. Sago came to Florida to close a business deal with a man. This man's arrival has been delayed a few days. To pass the wait time, Mr. Sago has taken to spending evenings dining at a local nightclub and gambling at a nearby casino. The casino is located on the reservation of the Pyanese Nation of Florida. I am sure you can see how this would be incredibly beneficial to us."

11

"No," Molka said. "But the neophyte in me needs to know."

"The laws are somewhat convoluted, but in the United States the Native American Nations have some quasi form of sovereignty. We will use this sovereignty and the assistance of a contractor team to facilitate our goal. Do you understand now?"

"I think you're saying that when Sago's at this reservation casino he's theoretically left the United States?"

"Precisely," Azzur said. "Casino security cameras will show Mr. Sago entering the Pyanese Nation and leaving United States soil, as our American friends wish, alive and coherent. At least enough to satisfy their plausible deniability requirements."

"But," Molka said, "casino security cameras won't show Sago returning to United States soil with the contractor team, bagged, gagged, and ready for shipment."

Azzur stubbed out his cigarette. "No one will ever see that. Again, plausible deniability."

Molka shook her head. "What would the world be like without the phony concept of plausible deniability?"

"Unworkable."

"So, it seems the poor Pyanese are going to take all the flack for Sago's mysterious disappearance in their nation."

"Regrettably. But in a few months, an associate will present a large donation to their tribal welfare fund."

"Backdoor guilt money," Molka said. "Nice touch."

"Now, you may be thinking, what about the other less than sympathetic countries, meeting in that big building in Manhattan, who will undoubtedly get around to asking our government, by way of condemning it, what they know about the 'Sago Affair?'"

Molka mimicked thoughtful. "Yes, I was just about to ask you that. Because your tedious geopolitical lectures are a major turn on for me."

"My lectures were actually on the nuances of global stratagems. But what do you think our government's response will be to their condemning questions?"

"Hmm…let me think. Would that be…um…um…plausible deniability, Azzur?"

"Must I always be a target for your sarcasm?"

Molka smiled. "Yes, you must."

"Your task is as follows: Make contact with Mr. Sago. Gain his trust, by any means necessary. Obtain an invitation to accompany him to the casino, by any means necessary. At the casino, detach Mr. Sago from his security and deliver him to the contractor team for processing."

"And what about his security?"

"Just one. He is called Maur. A former Greek wrestling champion and perhaps army special forces. We do not have a file on him. And the associates I asked to assist have not been unable to find much more information beyond that. Since Mr. Sago feels he only needs one man though, best to be most careful with him. Do you understand your task?"

Molka stood. "Yes. I understand I'm to be the arm candy for your rat trap." She capped her water, replaced it in the refrigerator, sat back at the table, and folded her arms, silent.

"What bothers you?" Azzur said.

"You don't use a high-performance race car for a ride sharing service."

"Meaning what?"

"Meaning this time, I was hoping for something a little more...high priority."

"Everything I give you is high priority."

Molka rested her chin on her fist. "I'll bet you say that to all your projects. But can't the contractor team just snatch him on their own?"

"They were not contracted for surveillance nor dealing with security threats. They are simply package processors."

"Guess you get what you pay for."

"Or overpay for," Azzur said. "No one has failed to take advantage of our present difficulties."

"Don't you have any younger, sluttier, more beautiful projects who can handle this?"

"Younger, yes. Sluttier, unknown. More beautiful? Debatable. Positively, none more qualified. If a desirable woman were to approach Mr. Sago in a nightclub or casino, he would instantly be suspicious of their motives. You have seen his undesirable face and so has he. However, if the beautiful veterinarian, the compassionate caretaker of his adored children, should offer herself for his accompaniment, what is there for him to be suspicious of?"

"I suppose." Molka flexed both hands. Soreness had set in. "But going behind the Americans' backs, significant friends of ours and otherwise, I don't like it. I don't think they're going to like it either."

"Nor do the Counsel. But as I said, Mr. Sago will be called into account."

"Someone once told me that if revenge is your motive, you should dig two graves—one for yourself."

"And I stand by that," Azzur said. "While Mr. Sago has contributed to the deaths of many of our people, we must find out what else he may know, who employed him, and what they have planned for us next. The Counsel is certain something much more devastating is coming. Therefore, he will first be obliged to save lives before any retribution is considered."

Molka studied Sago's photo again. "He has to suspect we're coming for him."

"He has dropped his guard for the moment. His arrogance, I spoke of, will doom him. For years he has gotten away with fraudulent deals, usually without the victim ever realizing it. He did not leave his home country in the year since he participated in our betrayal. But he now feels safe enough to have done so. The Counsel has determined that Mr. Sago believes he can make one last lucrative deal in the United States and retire to safety before we notice—if we ever do—his involvement with the Traitors."

"What's the time limit on this task?"

Azzur lit another cigarette. "You will have eight days upon your arrival tomorrow."

"Not a lot of time to meet him, gain his trust, and have him ask me out for a night at the casino."

"In eight days, Mr. Sago returns to Budapest. His personal pilot has already filed the flight plan. We cannot touch him in Hungary, even in our best times. He is too well protected by his good friend, the Strongman of the East."

Molka eyed Azzur. "Sago's tight with the Strongman of the East? Messing with the Strongman's friends is usually fatal." She smiled. "Maybe this really is high priority."

14

"The highest. This will be our only opportunity to get Mr. Sago. *You* are our only opportunity. If you fail, it is a certainty that many more will die."

"Alright. I'll do my best." Molka slid the tablet over to herself and swiped.

"Questions?" Azzur said. "Would you like me to go over it again?"

Molka caught him lusting her bare legs. "No questions. Looks like everything I need is here. You can leave. I know you're a man with much on his mind."

Azzur consulted his watch. "I do not report in for two hours. I could stay with you until then?"

"No, that's ok." Molka stretched her tee shirt to cover more of her thighs and yawned. "I want to go back to bed. I'm still tired. I had a rough night."

"Yet, perhaps not as rough a night as the two men you put to sleep in the parking lot."

Molka pushed the tablet away. "And again, I have no secrets from you."

"I understand these men woke up in the city hospital."

"Better for them to wake up in the city hospital than not wake up in the city morgue."

"That was your intention?"

"That was my mistake."

Azzur laughed. "Once in the Unit, always in the Unit, right? But now you must learn my ways, Molka. Controlled violence—very useful. Uncontrolled violence—very dangerous."

# CHAPTER THREE

Molka occupied an Economy Class window seat, the best a humble veterinarian should be able to afford. After takeoff, she declined a snack and viewed dawn breaking over the blue Mediterranean passing below. She checked the old pilot's watch on her left wrist. Right on time. The flight from Ben Gurion International to Miami International was scheduled for sixteen hours and forty-minutes, with a one-hour and forty-minute layover in Madrid. Plenty of time for thinking. And thinking back. And thinking about telling a story she had never told anyone.

Maybe she could tell her new friend? The passenger who sat next to her. They seemed kind and innocent—like a loyal dog. Maybe they could understand her story? She looked out the window again and told them.

"Never liked flying over water. In my helicopter, I was always more frightened of crashing into the Med than into the desert or the side of some mountain. The whole drowning thing really scares me. That's another story for another time. But speaking of crashing, my instructors at military flight school were afraid I would crash one of their precious training copters. Probably because I was the only female in the class. But when I graduated as top pilot, they painted 'Molka' on one of the copters as a tribute to me. They even invited me to come back and address the next class, which contained three females. I never got to give the speech I wrote. Because the Unit wanted me, and I wanted the Unit."

"What's the Unit, you say? Special Forces, and I'll just leave it at that."

"The missions. So many missions. Missions no school child will ever be taught to remember. Missions I can't teach myself to forget. The mission that cost me my little Janetta."

"Then came the American Captain. The beautiful man. The joint training exercises during the day, making love on the beach at night. Those were my last joyous days. He's the one who told me to get out of the Unit. That the missions would destroy me like they destroy everyone, especially if you survive them. So, I got out. And he was happy. And I was happy. And we were happy. And then he went back home. Back home, like all married men eventually do, to his wife and child. And I was left to forget the only man I've ever loved."

"I chose veterinary medicine as my post military career because animals don't lie to you, and they don't leave you. They die like people do, but you can get another one who loves you just as much. I still can't bring myself to own a pet though. I graduated early. Then I had my little practice and my clients and my life to live out quietly. I wasn't thirty yet."

"The Traitors Scandal changed all that. You probably heard about it. No? Well, it was the biggest security breach in the history of my country. Maybe in any country at any time. Moles burrowed in deep for ten years popped up and exposed the identity of almost every covert operative employed by the Counsel."

"The Counsel is what we call our intelligence service, by the way."

"Most of the Traitors were taken out by the military, but the damage they left behind was catastrophic. I guess you know my country has many enemies sworn to annihilate us. So the safeguarding role of covert operations is indispensable. The majority of the exposed operatives were immediately killed or went missing and are presumed dead. The few who made it home are in hiding or took early retirement or are writing books and appearing on talk shows. Obviously, they are of no more use for covert operations though. Like our prime minister said, the tip of the spear wasn't just blunted; the head of the spear was cut off and melted down."

"The military and internal security helped pick up some of the slack, but they were up to their helmets and shields in border threats. Our friends around the world publicly expressed their concern and sympathy, while privately expelling our operatives from their countries. We were very alone and very vulnerable."

"Needless to say, the Counsel was in panic mode. In the short term they tried using a few uncompromised retired operatives to fill in as best they could, along with some mid-level managers—bureaucrats—never qualified for field work. The results were disappointing, to put it nicely. In the long term, a new generation of operatives will be recruited and trained, but that will take several years. It's the time in between, right now, when we're in the most danger."

"The solution the Counsel came up with was Operation Civic Duty, more often called the Projects Program. The recruitment of ordinary citizens with some applicable skill or skills that can be utilized. Each citizen, or project as they're called, is given some quick, very basic, training then sent straight out to complete what the Counsel calls a task. Yes, I know it sounds desperate and borderline suicidal, because it is. Even so, they find willing projects everywhere. In the universities, the factories, athletes, scientists, housewives."

"But the Counsel told me I was their prize."

"Actually, it was their best recruiter, Azzur, who told me that when he showed up at my office. He said I not only possessed a useful skill set; I also had an excellent cover. Because who could be suspicious of a person who lives to be kind to animals? He told me the Counsel very much needed my help. I told him I was a patriot, but I had already done my duty. I wasn't interested. He smiled and left."

"He came back a week later with more information for me. Azzur can always find out more information. He told me all about my worst mission. How that mission caused the loss of my little Janetta. He said the Counsel knew the identity of the one responsible, and they knew where this one was hiding. And if I completed ten tasks for them, my eleventh task could be personal. They would give me the identity and location of the one. The one I would die to kill."

"I agreed to serve Azzur. I became his project: Project Molka."

"I completed my first task. I made mistakes, and there were some unfortunate consequences. Azzur was not pleased with my performance. But he also understands that I'm not one of the formally trained operatives he's used to working with. He told me there would be growing pains, and if I didn't get myself killed, I might become very good at it."

"Yesterday, I told Azzur I wouldn't assassinate or murder for him. I lied. I just tell him that to make myself feel like he doesn't have as much control over me as he thinks. Then again, I wasn't lying. Because I'm really not doing anything for him. I'm doing everything for her. And I will assassinate or murder or worse for her."

"I don't know if what Azzur told me about Mr. Gaszi Sago is true. I do know that if I give him to the Counsel, he will ultimately die. But if giving him to them brings me a task closer to the one who took my little Janetta, then Mr. Gaszi Sago will have to die."

"You understand, don't you?"

Molka turned back to her new friend, the passenger who sat next to her.

There was no new friend.

There was no passenger next to her.

There never was.

She sat alone.

Thinking.

PROJECT MOLKA: TASK 2
DAY 1 OF 8

CHAPTER FOUR

Molka arrived in Miami, cleared immigration and customs, found the black Mazda leased in her name in the airport parking garage, and drove to her apartment. The one bedroom one bath townhouse, located in a nice pastel building, was fully furnished as promised. It retained the regular resident's scent—menthol cigarettes with a hint of poodle—and she would reclean the refrigerator and reconfigure the furniture into a more efficient arrangement. Otherwise, it was acceptable.

In the bedroom dresser top drawer, Molka located her weapons: a Beretta 96A1 and a little "Baby Glock" 26. She had gained a fondness for the Beretta from her American Captain, although she chose to up caliber from 9mm to .40 S&W. In the second drawer, she found two boxes of ammunition for each pistol, and shoulder and small-of-the-back holsters for the Beretta. She tried on both. The small-of-the-back was preferable. She tucked the Glock into a small black purse, which came with a red cocktail dress in the closet. The closet held a complete wardrobe indeed, all in her size and close to her taste. The associates did their jobs well.

It was no surprise though. The associates always impressed. They were ordinary sympathetic citizens all over the world who provided the Counsel with information, obtained weapons, lent their apartment to someone they would never meet, and even shopped for clothes not in their size or style. Unlike a contractor team—mercenary specialists well compensated for their services—the associates worked only for the greater good of the cause. The Counsel couldn't survive without them.

Molka craved a nap. She needed a sleep catch-up after Azzur's early intrusion the previous morning and the fatiguing flight. Instead she showered, dressed in office attire, replaced her contacts with glasses, ponytailed her hair, and headed to the hospital.

The Kind Kare Animal Hospital resided in a pink stucco building on a palm lined boulevard. It looked nicer than any animal hospital Molka had ever seen, and nicer than many human hospitals she had seen too. No wonder: it served the affluent beach community of Cinnamon Cove.

After the hospital manager welcomed her, took her on a tour, and made staff introductions, Molka asked if she could take some appointments. The stated reason: to familiarize herself with hospital routines and procedures. The real reason: Sago's appointment the next day. She didn't want to look like a complete newbie to him.

Molka organized the instruments in a gleaming examination room that smelled of antiseptic. A college-aged female vet tech in turquoise scrubs knocked and entered. "Uh, yes, Doctor, uh...uh...I'm sorry; your last name is hard for me to pronounce."

"Molka is fine."

"Ok, cool. A Mr. and Mrs. Langley are here. They said there's a problem, and they have some important questions. They asked to talk to you specifically. They brought their yellow Lab. By the way, he's really cute. And so is their Lab."

Molka let the remark pass. "Bring them back."

A yellow Labrador on a leash nosed into the examination room, followed by the vet tech and a pair of American fashion models who had just left one of the nearby country clubs, or at least they looked that way to Molka. Both wore tennis whites; the woman molded into a short tight skirt and the man short tight shorts.

The woman appeared about Molka's age, height, and fitness, but she filled out a couple of sizes fuller in the bust and hips. Her blonde hair was cut shoulder length, and her eyes were Nordic blue.

Molka gauged the man as in his mid-thirties, around six feet three, and although not a bodybuilder, also not unfamiliar with the weight room. His brown hair was trimmed military style, and he had the type of deep-set brown eyes and strong jawline Molka found intriguing.

"Good afternoon," Molka said. "A fine-looking animal. What's his name?"

The couple looked at each other and back at Molka. The woman said, "I'll say, Yellow Dog."

The vet tech and Molka put on latex gloves and lifted the Lab onto the examination table. Molka took the dog's temperature with an ear thermometer, noted a normal reading, and proceeded to examine the nose, teeth, eyes, and ears. Then she said, "Any weight gain, weight loss, coughing, or unusual scratching?"

"I couldn't tell you," the woman said.

"Has he been eating normally?"

The woman shrugged. "I wouldn't know."

Molka put a stethoscope to the dog's chest. "Any diarrhea or other irregularities with his stool?"

The woman raised her eyebrows. "I definitely wouldn't know that."

Molka checked the dog's legs, paws, and abdomen, gave him a rewarding pat, and addressed the couple. "I find this animal to be in normal health. You said there was a problem with him? What do you think it is?"

The woman smiled. "I have no idea. Probably nothing. On the other hand, I only met him an hour ago."

Molka removed the latex gloves and washed her hands in a side sink. "Then how can I help you, Mr. and Mrs. Langley?"

"We rarely go by Langley," the woman said. "I'm Nadia. My partner is Warren."

"Nice to meet you, Nadia," Molka said and looked at the man. She liked the way he looked back. "And you as well, Warren."

"A pleasure," Warren said.

Molka turned to the vet tech. "We're finished here. You may go."

The vet tech helped the dog down, smiled at Warren when she handed him the leash, and left.

Molka shut the door. "I understand you also have some questions for me?"

"Just one," Nadia said. "What time today will you be leaving for home?"

"The hospital closes at six, so I suppose I will leave about—"

"I mean back home, home. Where you came from."

"I do not understand. I only arrived today. I am part of a veterinarian exchange program. If you are from immigration, my papers are in order."

"You can thin out the accent," Nadia said. "The Corporation knows who you really are, and why you're really here."

"I am sorry," Molka said. "I am confused. What is this corporation of which you speak?"

Molka's confused act was a defense mechanism. She knew the Corporation was the internal nickname for the central intelligence service in the US. Azzur often raved to her with envy about their seemingly unlimited resources as compared to their much smaller counterpart the Counsel. But they weren't responsible for domestic security. How did they know who she was and why had they come to burn her cover story?

"Cut the confused act," Nadia said. "You know all about the Corporation."

"And who are you?" Molka said.

Nadia smiled. "We're just a couple of lowly, devoted corporate minions."

Warren said to Nadia, "Admit I was right. She's stunningly perfect for the job."

Nadia hit Warren with annoyance. "Don't start, Warren." She looked back to Molka. "Warren and I have had the Honey Pot debate many times. I say it's been too overused to be effective. Warren says it's overused because it still works, and if you find the right pot for the honey, the horny bear will always eat it up."

Molka said, "Did you know both brown and black bears will raid beehives? They will also consume the bees and larvae inside, which are a good source of protein."

"But she's not here to seduce Sago," Nadia said. "I see that now. He's a late-middle aged billionaire. Waves of gold-digging tramps have come at him for years. He won't fall for that anymore. Instead, he's going to come sweep her off her feet."

"How do you figure?" Warren said.

Nadia pointed at Molka. "Look at the staging. The beautiful innocent foreign girl, all alone in a strange country. So vulnerable. So desirable. Caring for Sago's adored dogs. He won't be able to help himself. She plays it aloof and uninterested at first, to make him want her even more, but soon his worldly charm and blinding wisdom will win her over. And within a few months, he will tell her everything she was sent to find out and a hell of a lot more. Then she gets homesick, they part amicably, and Sago's left with a nice memory. Right up until the cleaning service arrives. It's a brilliantly conceived op."

Warren nodded. "Her people are the best at these."

"And I believe it could have worked," Nadia said. "Except she doesn't have a few months. Does she, partner?"

"He is your partner?" Molka said. "Does this mean he is also your husband? He would make a fine husband. A strong and handsome man."

Nadia flashed a noxious grin. "Aren't you the sweet little kitty cat? Warren, take the dog and go wait in the car. I want to talk to this *ketzelah* alone."

"Goodbye, handsome Warren," Molka said. "Perhaps I will see you on the beach sometime? I understand the beaches here are quite beautiful. And some, I am told, do not require a woman to wear her top."

Warren smiled. "Definitely something to think about. Goodbye, Molka."

Nadia glared Warren out the door, closed it, and aimed her glare at Molka. "Why don't you drop the quaint immigrant bullshit so you and I can come to an understanding."

"I don't understand anything you have said."

"Keep playing your role, but you're still going to listen to me. I'm sure they've told you Sago's private Airbus A350 is parked at the South Florida Regional Executive Airport. And seven days from two o'clock this afternoon, he's scheduled to board that big gaudy bitch and take off for Budapest. But what they didn't tell you, and what I want you to understand, is that my partner and I will make sure Sago leaves on that aircraft as scheduled and unharmed."

Molka mimicked impressed. "This Mr. Sago must be a very important man."

"And just so you know how we personally feel about that fat piece of Slavic trash, if something unfortunate should happen to his aircraft after he leaves US airspace—like a wing falls off, or the starboard engine flames out, or a stray AMRAAM takes the damn thing down—we couldn't give a shit less. But that's not going to affect how ruthlessly and efficiently we do our jobs. Understand?"

"No, but I am still listening."

"In the next few days, you can try to honey Sago up, but he's not stupid. And you shouldn't be either. Because he'll burn you too. And then he'll put his Greek psycho to work on you. And trust me, *ketzelah,* you don't want that."

"Your concern for my safety is touching," Molka said. "So, you have come to warn me?"

"No. This is more of a professional courtesy call. You can save us the trouble of watching you and save yourself your dignity. In other words, just go home. Now do you understand me?"

"I wonder what the fine special agents of the National Investigation Branch would think about your Corporation's unauthorized activities here?"

Nadia smiled. "We let the boys and girls of the Branch think they're doing a great job."

"Do you happen to know if they have a field office in this area?"

"It's located at 2030 Southwest 145th Avenue. That's in Miramar. Ask for Special Agent Hopkins. Since you're an animal lover, you'll probably like him. He has a face and personality like the south end of a north bound jackass. But, getting back to our problem. I asked if you understood me?"

Molka folded her arms. "I've heard everything you said."

"Good. Two more things I want you to hear from me." Nadia put her hand on Molka's shoulder and squeezed, hard. "One, my partner is not my husband, not yet anyway." Nadia squeezed even harder. "And two, make sure you keep your top on around him."

Molka took off her glasses, laid them on the examination table, smiled, and said, "And now two things I want you to hear from me: One, I keep my top on for whom I like. And two, I'm not really the touchy-feely type."

Molka snatched Nadia's wrist, twisted her arm behind her back into an armlock, shoved her face first into the wall, and held her there.

Nadia's body tensed. "Impressive. You're fast. But you should have broken my arm when you had the chance."

Nadia leaned back, placed a foot with a bent knee waist high on the wall, and pushed with explosive power. She and Molka jetted across the room and mashed into a storage cabinet. It popped open and disgorged its contents. Molka lost the armlock and landed on her backside.

Nadia spun around and assumed a Muay Thai style fighting stance.

Molka jumped to her feet and assumed a fighting stance.

"Krav Maga?" Nadia said. "You want to kill me, *ketzelah?*"

Molka shifted her stance; Muay Thai. "Feel better, *kelba?*"

Nadia smiled. "Thank you."

Nadia slipped Molka's front kick.

Molka ducked Nadia's straight right jab.

Molka's right cross glanced off Nadia's cheek.

Nadia's knee speared Molka's ribs, followed by a straight left jab that missed, backing Molka into the instrument cart. It toppled with a rattling crash.

Molka's side kick connected with Nadia's ribs.

Nadia's left hook tagged Molka's left eye.

Molka's straight kick caught Nadia's lower lip.

Both fighters retreated to neutral room corners, panting. End of round one.

Nadia moved fast. Molka moved a little faster. Molka struck hard. Nadia struck a little harder.

It could go either way.

Nadia moved to strike again.

Molka readied herself.

There was a knock, and the vet tech opened the door and stepped in. "Mrs. Greenblatt's here. Her cat has ear mites again and she wants to know if—" She noted the disheveled fighters and the debris strewn floor. "Oh, wow. Oh, wow!"

Nadia smiled. "We just had a little disagreement over payment."

The vet tech said, "We, uh, take all major credit cards."

Molka moved face to face with Nadia. "There was no disagreement over payment. She's lying. She threatened me and provoked a fight."

"Oh man," the vet tech said. "Want me to call the police, Doctor, uh, Molka?"

"The police?" Molka said. "Yes; maybe we should expose her to the local authorities."

Nadia deferred in silence to Molka, the accused waiting for an unsure verdict.

"Ok," the vet tech said. "I'll go call them."

"No," Molka said. "That won't be necessary. Miss Nadia from Langley now understands how I react to threats and respond to a fight."

In the animal hospital parking lot, Nadia dropped into her driver's seat, and slammed the door. Warren waited in the passenger seat and the yellow Lab paced and panted on the backseat.

"Jeez," Warren said. "Your lip is bleeding. And you're sweating. What happened in there?"

"Nothing. I mean something. I mean she has some skills."

"I guess she's not leaving?"

Nadia checked her face in the rearview mirror and dabbed blood from her lip with a finger. "No."

"Ok. Which team do you want me to take off Sago and put on her? Lawn Service or Pest Control? I rate Pest Control as much better, by the way."

"Maybe neither. She pulled the Branch card on me."

"Smart girl," Warren said. "You call her on it?"

"Of course."

"But do you really think she would inform the Branch and burn us back?"

"Not unless she had to. That would be almost as messy for the Counsel as it would for the Corporation."

"Then Pest Control it is. I'll have them on her within the hour."

Nadia turned to Warren. "What's the one sure thing we know about leaks?"

"They always have more than one agenda behind them."

"Exactly. And the leak on her came a little too hard in an easy way."

"Think she's actually a distractor?"

"Distractor for a cleaning service?"

"Sure." Warren handed Nadia a wet wipe from the glovebox for her lip. "We divide our resources to keep track of her, and they slip in the backdoor. Or if she gets into Sago's house, she could leave the backdoor unlocked for them—literally."

"Her people have done some ballsy things in the past but taking out Sago after the Corporation asked them not to, that would be…pretty damn bad."

"Yes, it would. But international outrage isn't a high priority with their ops."

"That's true," Nadia said. "You really think…. Nah. We're over-analyzing again. Her people desperately want some enhanced discussion time with Sago. If they wanted him gone, they would've splashed him in the Atlantic on the way over here. I think we should proceed as planned. Keep all resources on Sago. Let her play with him for a few days if it makes her people feel better. Besides, now that she knows she's burnt, she won't do anything too crazy. Agreed?"

"Agreed."

"Good." Nadia started the car. "Let's go return this mutt to the pet store."

PROJECT MOLKA: TASK 2
DAY 2 OF 8

CHAPTER FIVE

Molka winced her way through an early morning run. She and the swishing lawn sprinklers were the only ones awake in the neighborhood. Hopefully the physical activity would work out the soreness from Nadia's beating. And hopefully a heavy make-up application and her glasses would cover the bruise under her left eye. It was the best she could do in the time left before Sago's 10:00AM appointment.

The vet tech reported the scuffle to the hospital manager. Molka told the manager Nadia was a former opponent from her collegiate martial arts days, and the fight was only some friendly sparring that got out of hand. The manager said she would accept the preposterous lie because, "Lies are more tolerable than scandals in a place like Cinnamon Cove." Made sense.

Nadia and Warren puzzled her though. They were not the lowly devoted corporate minions they claimed to be. More like highly skilled and experienced combatants. A nasty surprise to be sure, and obviously the "significant American friends of ours" Azzur talked about was the Corporation. But how they found out about her so quickly was for the Counsel to investigate, not her. She had followed her instructions precisely. Nadia and Warren knew who she was but were wrong about why she was there. She would try to use that to her advantage. She also figured their threat of putting her under surveillance was a bluff. Corporation employees watching one foreign national—Sago—on US soil stepped on the Branch's jurisdictional toes, ego, and ire in a major way to begin with. The Corporation wouldn't risk getting caught watching another foreigner behind their backs, much less one sent by the Counsel. And with inter-agency rivalries being what they were, they probably wouldn't tell the Branch about her either. All things considered; she was not in bad shape.

Even so, her limited training and lifelong instincts told her to abort the task. She had been compromised, and it couldn't be safely completed. As Nadia suggested, she should just go home. But if she did, the Counsel would never give her another task, and she needed nine more to get to the task she wanted. She would go forward.

7:45AM: Molka arrived at the Kind Kare Animal Hospital.
8:15AM: Molka vaccinated a Seal Point Himalayan kitten.
8:50AM: Molka examined a Boston Terrier and gave a new diet recommendation.
9:20AM: Molka removed sutures from an adorable Chihuahua named Maximo.
9:40AM: Molka applied more make up in the bathroom mirror. Her black eye was barely visible.
9:46AM: Molka took up an observation position at the receptionist's desk near the front door.

She watched the door and made small talk with the receptionist while a package was delivered. The receptionist handed the package to Molka; it was for her. Molka took the tablet sized box and read the return address: ICM Electronics, Lowell, Massachusetts.

Molka sat in one of the waiting area chairs and opened the box. It did contain a tablet. She powered up the device and entered the password she had been assigned by Azzur. The desktop displayed two things: a single folder and a countdown clock already counting down from fifteen minutes. She knew from previous Azzur briefing tablets the hard drive would be scrubbed when the clock reached zero. She clicked on the folder. A PowerPoint presentation opened.

The first slide displayed: a black background with white text: "Lest you be charmed by the fat snake, behold his venom's victims. A small sample of the covert operatives exposed by the Traitors with the help of Mr. Gaszi Sago."

The next slide displayed: a headshot taken from a young man's government ID badge. Under the smiling face was the name "Aaron." Under that, text reading: "Age 24. Linguistics Analyst, Embassy, Paris, France. Went missing on 05/30. Castrated male testicles found in his apartment's bathroom sink later identified through DNA as his. Remainder of body still missing."

The next slide: a headshot of a pleasant plump faced middle-aged man. "Joel. Age 56. Passport Office Director, Consulate-General, São Paulo, Brazil. On 11/21 shot twenty-one times by rider and passenger on a motorcycle as he exited a local ice cream shop. Perpetrators unknown. Left behind seven daughters and thirteen grandchildren."

The next slide: a headshot of an attractive woman. "Emmanuella. Age 31. Community Liaison Coordinator, Embassy, Ashgabat, Turkmenistan. On 09/05 found in her rented suburban home beaten, raped, hanged, and shot in the head. Death ruled a probable suicide by local authorities. Was to be married the next month."

Forty-seven more slides remained in the presentation. Molka had seen enough. It was an effective technique. In the Unit, the Major sometimes showed the assault teams gruesome HD blowup photos of their target's victims. Afterwards, they were always certain of what they had to do. Azzur wanted to make sure she was certain too.

9:57AM: A six-foot five-inch rectangular armor block, like a main battle tank stood on edge, breached the hospital's main entrance; it was Sago's one-man security force: Maur.

His brown crewcut glinted gray at the temples, but his tight-cut black suit showed the former wrestling champion had lost little power and muscle to early middle age. He removed his sunglasses and scanned the lobby-waiting area. His dark eyes chilled Molka. They seemed incapable of sympathy.

Maur held the door and a man entered. Molka's first impression: The photos she had seen did him no justice. Gaszi Sago was much more disturbing in person—not uglier, more disturbing, because he looked so harmlessly weak.

His dyed blond hair horseshoed around baldness. The face beneath it sagged under the eyelids and at the jowls. A tailored cobalt blue silk Italian suit did not flatter him as it did his man Maur. It exposed a portly body long devoid from meaningful exercise. Molka found it unusual he wore no jewelry though, since he could afford the best. He led a stunning matched pair of black and white Löwchens wearing diamond-studded collars attached to gold chain leashes.

Like most animals, Sago's dogs were drawn to Molka. She rose from the chair and knelt to pet them.

Sago fixated on Molka. "I see my Artemis and Apollo favor you."

"They're gorgeous," Molka said. "And so sweet."

"Thank you, doctor. Will you be handling the examination of my children this morning?"

"Yes, if you wish."

Sago smiled. "I insist. Your accent. You are Israeli?"

Molka stood. "I am."

"I have always believed the women of the Middle East to be the most mysterious and beautiful. You have certainly proven me correct again. I have done much trading in your country. I am guessing you are from Haifa?"

"Close. Kiryat Bialik. But I spent most of my childhood in Haifa."

"Then Haifa's loss is Cinnamon Cove's and—more importantly—my gain." He took Molka's right hand and with a deep bow kissed it. "I am Gaszi Sago, your servant."

"I am Molka. And I am impressed and charmed."

She lied about the first thing but wasn't sure about the second.

Sago swept a hand toward Maur. "And this is my valued assistant, Maur."

Molka smiled. "Good morning, Maur."

Maur acknowledged her with silent dark eyes.

Molka turned to Sago. "Shall we go to the examination room?"

With the vet tech assisting, Molka gave the dogs a standard examination. Sago stood watching, too close, his expensive English cologne overpowered the room. Maur kept vigil outside the open door.

Molka finished, dismissed the vet tech, and said, "Mr. Sago, I'm happy to inform you, your animals are in perfect health."

"But I will only be truly happy if you consent to call me Gaszi. May I also ask, what brings you to this country?" Sago's smile went sly. "You do not hide from a dark past, do you?"

"No. I'm part of a veterinarian exchange program. My stay here is only temporary."

"I see. You came with your husband? He awaits you back home?"

Molka forged bashfulness. "No husband."

"Of course! A beauty like you has many boyfriends to spoil her. I cannot fault you for this."

"No boyfriends either."

"So, you are here alone?"

Molka forged humbleness. "I am."

"Unacceptable! Let us become friends. I usually dine at The Indigo Club. It is what they call a gentleman's club in this country. I enjoy the ambiance there. Join me tonight for dinner and pleasant commiseration, as we are but two strangers in a strange land."

"That's very nice of you. But I must decline."

"We'll talk of your wonderful Haifa! We'll talk of the food, the culture, the Bahá'í Gardens, the gold-domed Shrine of the Báb! We'll talk of the beaches of Hof HaCarmel! The Wadi!"

"Mr. Sago, you're making me homesick."

And he was.

"We'll talk of my children and the children we may someday have together! Say you will dine with me tonight!"

"I'm sorry, Mr. Sago. I really couldn't."

36

"Your answer is final?"

"Today, yes."

"Today, yes?" Sago said. "Ah, today, yes. I understand. You wish to play. Very well. The ancient game of seduction is commenced." He smiled. "However, I am an accomplished player in my own right. Fair warning, fair lady."

Molka smiled. "I consider myself warned."

"For my opening gambit, I have just decided my children will require twice weekly check-ups in this hospital. Therefore, I will see you again in a few short days, perhaps?"

Molka forged playfulness. "Perhaps."

Sago took and kissed her hand again. "Farewell, beautiful one. Till next we meet."

"Good day, Mr. Sago." Sago frowned. "I mean, Gaszi." He bowed and left with his dogs trailed by Maur.

Gaining his trust had been easier than she imagined. She would have preferred to spurn his advances for a few weeks though, turning her rejection into his obsession. Then he would have followed her anywhere. Then she could have led him anywhere. She knew how to play the ancient game of seduction too. But there was no time for the game, no time to wait for his next move. The next night she would go to him.

PROJECT MOLKA: TASK 2
DAY 3 OF 8

CHAPTER SIX

"All brass and high-class ass," is how The Indigo Club owner described his establishment. His assertion was half true. Both claims were supported by a heavy dose of indigo wallpaper, carpet, and lighting. A DJ booth overlooked three stages for the fifty or so girls dancing on a given night. And in the far back corner an indigo door led to the VIP Suites, where sullied dreams became sullied reality.

9:06 PM: Molka stood at the bar with a bottled water surveying for Sago. No sighting yet. The place was packed, and the music thumped loud. She had bypassed all the short dresses in her closet and chosen a slim-cut black Prada pants suit, not so much to continue the demure act for Sago, but because the jacket, when worn open, covered her Beretta in the behind-the-back holster clipped to her belt. Bringing a weapon into a nightclub illegally was not a good idea. But with Maur near, it somewhat reassured.

Two guys next to Molka tried three times to buy her a drink. They gave up and staggered away, their places taken by a skinny drunk guy and a busty dancer in pink pasties and a G-string. He ordered a shot he didn't need.

With his back to Molka, the drunk said to the dancer, "Damn Solana, why you got to be such a bitch all the time?"

The dancer said, "And why do you have to be a cheating asshole who doesn't take care of his kid?"

The drunk backhanded the dancer hard upside her cheek. The dancer stood mortified, touching his red handprint.

Now why did he have to do that?

"Just put some ice on it and shut up," he said to the dancer and downed his shot.

And why did he have to say that?

Molka tapped the drunk on the shoulder. He turned around. She backhanded him hard upside his cheek and said, "The humiliation stings more than the slap, doesn't it?"

"Damn bitch! You crazy!"

He swung a slap at Molka, but she blocked it with her forearm, backhanded him hard upside his cheek again, and said, "Just put some ice on it and shut up."

The dancer pushed in between the drunk and Molka. "Why you wanna fuck wit my baby's daddy?"

"I could ask you the same question," Molka said. "But it's fine, sweetie. No need to thank me."

"Go thank your momma."

"Does your momma know what you do for a living?"

The dancer's face turned perplexed. "Hell yeah, she dances dayshift here."

A baritone voice from behind said, "Ok, Mr. Slapper and Miss Slapper, you're both out of here. Solana, go back to work."

Molka turned around to see the source of the voice. Three huge bouncers arrived on the scene. All wore jeans and black t-shirts with SECURITY written across the front. The white letters glowed indigo from the décor.

The biggest, the one who did the talking, who Molka identified as the head bouncer, exhibited Pacific Islander origins. No older than twenty-five, he stood about six-foot-three and carried at least three hundred and forty-pounds of muscle and bulk. He grew a chin-only goatee and flaunted thick black hair pulled into a flowing ponytail.

"Hold up, cuz," the drunk said. "You can't kick me out. This crazy bitch hit me. I wasn't doing nothing, cuz."

"That's what they all say to me," the head bouncer said. "We're going to escort you to your cars and see you off the premises via the back exit. Garbage goes out with the garbage."

Molka estimated the distance to the front door for running escape purposes—her concealed weapon without a permit possibly becoming unconcealed by the bouncers the reason. It would not have been too difficult. Those big boys could never catch her. But she considered that she might have to come there again to meet Sago. Better to play it compliant.

"I'm very sorry," Molka said to the head bouncer. "I didn't come here to start any trouble."

He said, not sympathetic, "That's what they all say to me. Let's go."

The head bouncer put the drunk before him, Molka behind him, and the other two bouncers behind her. He led them around the bar and through a door marked "No Admittance." It opened onto a hallway. The club music muffled and faded when the door shut behind them. The hallway ended at another door under a red exit sign.

"Damn, cuz," the drunk said to the head bouncer. "You better stop pushing me, cuz."

The head bouncer said, "And you better stop slow walking me. Because I'm about to stop pushing and start snapping my boot off in your skinny behind...cuz."

"I'm telling you don't put your hands on me again, cuz. I'm serious, cuz."

The head bouncer opened the exit door onto a lighted back lot. Dumpster aroma offended nostrils.

The drunk stopped in the doorway and said, "I should at least get my cover charge back, cuz. This ain't right, cuz."

The head bouncer's right paw-hand grabbed the drunk's upper arm and walk-carried him out the door. Molka followed, with the other bouncers still behind her.

"Let me tie my shoe, cuz," the drunk said. "I'm going to trip and fall the way you keep pushing me, cuz."

The head bouncer stopped. "Quickly."

The drunk dropped to his left knee. Molka watched him pull up his right pants cuff. Slip on shoes. No laces to tie. Something attached to his ankle. She leapt away from her escorts and

41

thunked a roundhouse kick to his head. He crumpled over on his left hip, open mouthed and unconscious.

The head bouncer flexed into fight mode, but with the fight already over, he relaxed. The other two bouncers moved up and grabbed Molka's arms. One said to the other, "Did you see how fast she was?"

The head bouncer analyzed Molka, looked down at the drunk, back up at Molka, and sighed. "You couldn't have waited to do that until he was off our property? Now he'll probably sue us for not protecting him from you."

Molka pointed. "Check his right ankle."

The head bouncer crouched, patted the drunk's right ankle, lifted the pants leg, and exposed an ankle holster. He removed a small black semi-automatic pistol and stood.

"Holy shit," one of the other bouncers said.

The head bouncer held the pistol up to the light. "Ruger LC9." He released the magazine. "Loaded too."

"Holy shit," the other bouncer said.

The head bouncer addressed his men. "Tote cuz here into the storage room. Search him good when you get in there, and then call the cops. I'll be along in a minute. I want to talk to the lady first."

The bouncers lifted the drunk at the shoulders and ankles and carried him back inside.

The head bouncer examined the pistol again, made it safe, and tucked it into his front pocket. "I've told the owner we need metal detectors at the front door. He says that would look too ghetto. Maybe so. But he's not the one who's going to get capped by some drunk punk. He was really going for that little nine. He could have killed my guys—or me. Thanks. I owe you one."

"Don't think of it," Molka said.

"You've got a good eye. How did you see it anyway?"

"I was in the military in my home country. We were trained to look for such things."

The head bouncer nodded, impressed. "Might also explain the vicious roundhouse you gave him. By the way, what are you carrying?"

"Excuse me?"

He pointed at her back. "I saw your small-of-the-back holster at the bar. I've also got a pretty good eye."

Molka gave him the scared timid woman cliché look. "As I said, I don't want any trouble. Can I please just leave?"

The head bouncer held up a hand. "Hey, I'm all about concealed carry. I've got my license too. I guarantee that punk doesn't have his though. I think anyone who wants to should legally carry to protect themselves. Especially women alone. And especially, especially women alone who look like you. So, it's cool."

"Thank you."

"And may I also ask what a woman who looks like you is doing here alone?"

"I came here to meet someone," Molka said. "Maybe you know him. Mr. Gaszi Sago?"

"Yeah, I know him. A real enema nozzle. Oh, excuse me. You're his date for the evening? Girlfriend?"

"No, we're not together. I just have some business with him."

"Just business. That's a relief. If you told me you were with him, I was going to give up all hope and start searching for a high bridge." The head bouncer smiled. "Joking. But that makes sense. He's been doing his business in here the last three weeks. Booked exclusive use of the VIP's VIP Suite. Takes ten girls at a time back there with him. He even has meals catered in by his personal chef. Real big shot, I guess."

"What's the VIP's VIP Suite?"

"It's a special suite with its own private entrance and parking area and no security cameras. You know, so very special VIPs can come and go without anyone—aka their wives—ever finding out."

"Sounds convenient," Molka said. "Is Mr. Sago in there now?"

"He should be. He came in about an hour ago."

"And I assume he's with his large companion?"

"Yeah, and his small one too."

"Who would the small one be?"

"Some guy named O'Donnell," The head bouncer said. "Old friend of Sago's or something. Showed up here last night. He's an enema nozzle too. And a tweeker. And a freak. Tells the girls he can get them any drug they desire and brags about these wild sex parties he has. He's already tried to roofie a couple of them too. Don't let him make you a drink."

"I won't. And thank you."

The head bouncer put his hand on the door jam and leaned relaxed. "You know, this Sago guy and this O'Donnell guy, with their fancy suits and VIP Suite and throwing around mega cash, remind me of this guy from New York who came in here once. He was grabbing the girls' butts on stage. Even though there's a huge sign by the stage that says you can't touch the dancers. Why do New Yorkers always think rules don't apply to them? I tell him to stop, he keeps doing it, so I bounced him. And what does he do when we get outside? He grabs my ponytail and starts hunching on me from behind saying, 'I paid twenty dollars to get in, and I'm getting twenty dollars' worth of ass before I leave, one way or another.' I waited for him to finish laughing. And then I explained to him our local economy is tourism based, so we greatly appreciate our northern visitors. But this is also our home. And he might consider keeping that in mind and showing a little more courtesy to us residents on his next visit."

"Good advice," Molka said. "Then you sent him on his way with no hard feelings?"

"No. Then I fractured his jaw and his collarbone and waited for the manager to call the paramedics. Damn dumb-ass New Yorkers. But I shouldn't say that. I'm sure most New Yorkers are fine people. And I try to love everyone. I'm just a humble man of peace."

Molka smiled. "No arguments here."

Maybe she could become friends with this guy. He reminded her of a chip off a mountain. Young, but not immature. Amiable. He also knew inside information on the club. Always look to recruit useful assets, Azzur told her. If she could make him like her too, he could be helpful in completing her task.

"I guess I'll be going," Molka said. "Maybe I'll see you again sometime, if I'm allowed to come back?"

"Come back anytime. But you're welcome to stay and do your business with old boy back there."

"You don't mind?"

"Not at all," the head bouncer said. "Better let me hold your weapon for you though. You don't want to lose your CW license. The owner here isn't a big Second Amendment guy. I'll lock it in the safe. You can pick it up from me when you leave."

Tough choice. She wanted a weapon in case Maur became a problem. But if she said no to the bouncer's request and left, he might get suspicious. Maybe even say something to Sago. She would have to risk it. She unclipped the holster from her belt and handed it to him.

The head bouncer smiled approval. "Sweet Beretta. Come on, I'll escort you to the VIP's VIP Suite. I have the secret door code."

"Thank you. I'm Molka, by the way. What's your name?"

"My real name is Loto, but everyone calls me Baby."

"Then I'll call you Loto."

Loto liked that.

CHAPTER SEVEN

The secret door code for the VIP's VIP Suite was:

KNOCK, KNOCK, KNOCK, KNOCK.

Pause.

KNOCK, KNOCK, KNOCK, KNOCK.

Loto explained the heavy hinge-rattling sequence, he called "a cop knock," signaled to the dancers inside that someone from the staff wanted them to get themselves and their clients legally presentable and open the door.

Loto applied the knock and left to take care of the little armed drunk problem. Molka stood waiting for the door to open. She expected to face the dark eyes of Maur, but instead faced the dark beauty of a naked girl who said, "Join the party, boo."

Molka stepped inside. The girl shut the door behind her. The loud music from the club was silenced; it was a sound-proofed room. Different music played at a lower volume. The dim lit spacious suite featured indigo carpeting, mahogany paneling, a leather sofa and chairs, a full bar, and a king-sized bed. Only the brass stripper pole in the middle distinguished it from an upscale hotel room.

Ten dancers in ten varieties of shape, color, and sobriety lounged on or around the couch at the far end. On the couch sat a thin, pale man.

The man's eyes lusted over Molka. "Well, well, the stripper wears Prada."

Molka scanned the suite. No Sago. No Maur.

"Excuse me," Molka said. "I'm looking for Mr. Sago. I understood he was here."

"He's already left me," the man said. "Gone to wager with the natives again. Come." He patted the leather next to him. "Sit and be nice to me instead."

About twenty-five years before, at about age twenty-five, he might have been an attractive man. But the following twenty-five years of too much tanning and peroxide and cigarettes and alcohol and cocaine and heroin and opiates had left him a decaying shell hiding in an expensive suit.

"I don't work here," Molka said. "I'm here at Mr. Sago's invitation."

The man smiled. "Typical Gaszi." He put his arms around the two dancers flanking him. "All these beautiful girls, and still not satisfied. He has to import more in."

"You've misunderstood me. I'm not in this...profession."

"Well, what *profession* are you in, baby? And more importantly, how much do you charge?"

Molka folded her arms. "I'm a veterinarian. And I get paid to fix sick animals. But make another remark like that, and I'll fix you for free."

The man laughed. "Meeeeeow!"

Molka moved toward the door.

"Hold on," the man said. "Don't be upset. You're a friend of Gaszi's? I am too. His good friend. Frank O'Donnell. You are?"

"Molka."

"Greetings, Molka. But I'm sure he's told you all about Fast Frankie here?"

"No, he hasn't."

O'Donnell laughed again. "Of course he hasn't. Gaszi doesn't like to share the good stuff. In any case, he would take it as a personal insult from us both if you didn't let me offer you a drink. Now, come join me."

It was a gross proposition but being polite to the friend of her target made sense. She could obtain whatever intel she could and politely get out. Molka sat on the couch next to O'Donnell.

"What's your pleasure?" O'Donnell said. "And I have everything that brings pleasure, alcohol and otherwise."

"Just a bottled water, please."

O'Donnell called to a dancer sitting at the bar, "Bottled water for the lady and another double for me." He turned back to Molka. "You really a veterinarian?"

"Yes."

"How do you know Gaszi?"

"I work at the hospital he brings his pets to."

"Well, I guess those damn dogs come in handy for something. Loves those dogs more than his wives. He's on the third versions of each since I've known him."

"You've been friends a long time?" Molka said.

"We've done business together for years. But now I'm going to miss him. Did he tell you he was retiring for good?"

"No. He didn't mention that either."

"It's true. I'll probably never see him again after this visit."

You can count on it—Fast Frankie.

The dancer handed O'Donnell a refill and handed a bottled water to Molka. When she left, Molka said, "What type of business are you and Mr. Sago involved in?"

O'Donnell hesitated his drink. "What's your interest in our personal business?"

"Nothing personal. I'm always interested in learning about the interesting professions of interesting people."

O'Donnell smiled. "You would be surprised at the interesting professional people I know." A new tune started. "I love this song! It's perfect for a lapdance. Girls, entertain our guest." He took the bottled water from Molka. "Go enjoy yourself."

Two nude dancers took Molka's hands and pulled her up. Another nude dancer placed a chair next to the stripper pole. They led Molka to the chair and sat her down. It was her first time in a gentlemen's club; she wasn't sure what they had in mind. They smiled, and she didn't feel threatened though; she kept being polite. All ten dancers, now nude, surrounded her, and took turns gyrating on her to the music.

Behind the wall of nudity, Molka could not see the syringe that O'Donnell took from his jacket pocket. Nor did she see him insert the thin needle into her water bottle just below the cap.

The song ended. The dancers dispersed. Molka sat alone. Enough politeness; it was time to go. She stood and said, "Thank you for the hospitality, Mr. O'Donnell. But I should be going. I have an early call at the hospital in the morning."

O'Donnell oversold disappointment. "Leaving me so soon? The real party hasn't even started yet."

"I'm sorry. And yes, I must. I'm not really much of a partier anyway."

"Very well, but before you leave, a toast." O'Donnell handed Molka back her water bottle. She inspected it. Still factory sealed. O'Donnell raised his glass. "To our generous host, soon to be gone, but never forgotten, Gaszi Sago."

O'Donnell and all the dancers drank up. Molka uncapped the bottle and joined the toast.

O'Donnell raised his glass again. "And a toast to the hot sluts of The Indigo Club! And to hot sluts everywhere!"

O'Donnell and all the dancers drank up again. Molka joined the toast again.

A dancer held something to O'Donnell's nose. He inhaled and jumped up on the couch. "I am the king of carnal desires and I command you all to dance! Dance, you sluts, dance!"

They all danced.

Dizziness hit Molka first, nausea came next. She wanted to go to the ladies' room and vomit. She moved toward it.

O'Donnell leapt off the couch and blocked her way. "Leaving?"

"Yes. I'm going to be sick."

"No, you're not. Ride it out. You'll feel much better in a second."

"I have to go."

"You're not going anywhere."

Molka's head twirled. She strived for balance. "Let me leave. Move away from the door. What are you doing?"

O'Donnell smiled. "You're almost there."

"Where?"

"You ready to have fun tonight, baby?"

"What?" Molka said. "What did you say? Wha—"

"I said, you ready to have fun tonight, baby?"

"Yes…I'll show how fun…I'm ready to have…you with."

Molka raised her leg to give him a side kick and toppled to the floor. O'Donnell laughed. She reached behind her for her weapon.

Where's my weapon?

She sat up disorientated.

I'm falling…falling…falling…through the floor. But how can I be falling when I'm not moving?

The girls dancing around her shimmered and doubled. She struggled to her feet, took a step, stumbled back, and landed on the couch. She tried to stand, and almost did, but O'Donnell sat next to her and put his arm around her shoulders, holding her down.

"Party's over girls," O'Donnell said. "Everyone leave. Now!"

The dancers got dressed and began to leave. Molka wanted to follow. She tried to follow, but she was not strong enough to move him.

Her mind fought her body; *stand up, get out.*

Her body fought her mind; *lie down, go to sleep.*

Her body won.

Molka's eyes closed.

Molka's eyes opened.

She was laying on endless red cushions. They filled a large room with mirrors for walls. She was nude.

She tried to move again. She could not move again. She was floating and falling and floating and falling. She tried to talk. She could not talk.

All around her, nude men and women were having sex in various combinations.

A man's hand was on her breast.

Another man moved between her legs.

Others watched and waited.

O'Donnell's face, behind his phone, hovered over her. He was videoing her and talking.

"That was quick. Who's next?"

It went on and on and on and on....

Molka wanted to fight. She couldn't fight.

She wanted to scream. She couldn't scream.

She wanted to cry. She couldn't cry.

She wanted to close her eyes. She couldn't close her eyes.

She tried to close them.

She fought to close them.

She asked them to close.

She pleaded with them to close.

She begged them to close.

Finally.

Molka's eyes closed.

CHAPTER EIGHT

Except for the college aged kid sitting in the stockroom on a stool in front of an unmarked door with an Uzi on his lap, the Day-Night store in the Kerem HaTeimanim section of Tel Aviv looked and operated as a normal neighborhood grocery. But located on the guarded door's other side was a fully equipped trauma center OR and ICU unit, complete with a nurse on 24-hour duty and twice daily visits from doctors and specialists.

At lunch time, Azzur entered the Day-Night, and walked past the check-out counter to the rear of the store and through a swinging door into the stockroom. He approached the Uzi kid and handed him an ID card. The kid checked the ID, handed it back to Azzur, looked up at a security camera across the room that pointed at the door, and nodded twice. The door opened with a loud click.

Azzur stepped through into a small room serving as a nurse's station. Behind a desk sat a young pretty female nurse watching several computer screens. Azzur gave her his ID and took out and handed over a Sig P226 pistol from an inside the waistband holster. The nurse took the pistol, checked and returned the ID, and pressed a hidden button. A door to Azzur's left opened and he went into the next room.

Jaron and Dov lay in hospital beds. Both were attached to multiple IV's and monitors, their broken noses in splints and their swollen and blackened eyes barely open. Dov's dual wrist casts were propped up on special holders attached to his bed. Jaron mouth breathed through the wires holding his jaw shut.

Azzur moved between the beds. He dropped a disgusted frown on Dov's casts. "Useless."

"I think I'll still be able to work with explosives," Dov said.

Azzur turned to Jaron. "And what do you have to say for yourself? Oh, my mistake. You cannot talk anymore, can you?"

Jaron nodded and picked up a white board and marker from a table next to his bed. He wrote and held it up for Azzur to read: "Thanks for getting us out of city hospital."

"Yes, thanks," Dov said. "That police detective wouldn't give up. He said sooner or later, when we felt better, we would have to tell him what happened."

"But you will tell me now." Azzur sat in a chair across the room and lit a cigarette. "Because my instructions for you were simple. Did I not make myself clear?"

Jaron nodded and Dov said, "Yes, clear. Absolutely clear."

"Then please repeat my instructions back to me, so we can both honestly say you are not a liar."

Dov said, "We got jobs at the warehouse next to her office. We were to make sure we were outside every morning when she arrived. We were to start by harassing her, increase the intensity over the next few weeks, provoke a confrontation, rough her up, threaten her with sexual assault, stop just short of actually doing it, and tell her next time that we wouldn't stop."

Azzur flicked ash on the floor. "You are not a liar. Those were my instructions. Yet, instead of successfully carrying them out, you both get your asses kicked to within an inch of death, and she is more emboldened than ever. So, before I lose my legendary cool and start disconnecting these machines or just go retrieve my pistol from the sexy big-titted girl in the next room, tell me what happened."

"Jaron was team leader," Dov said. "He should tell you."

Jaron erased his board with a sponge, wrote, and held it up again: "You didn't tell us about her Krav Maga skills."

"Don't you both also have Krav Maga skills?"

"Not like hers," Dov said. "But she caught us off guard, took us down with her first volley. The rest was just her having fun."

"Did she say anything prior to her having her fun?" Azzur said.

"Not at first. Jaron was trying to get her to answer a passive-aggressive question to scare and intimidate her, as you suggested."

"And what was her response?"

"She responded by asking us both a passive-aggressive question. Well, it was more like an aggressive-aggressive question. Because she backed up her questions to the letter."

"Did she say anything else? Anything more relevant to her situation?"

Dov thought a moment. "Yes. She said, nothing is decided until it's decided."

Azzur stood, tossed his cigarette on the tile floor, stamped it out, and moved toward the door.

"Jaron and I wanted to ask you something," Dov said.

Azzur stopped, turned, and read the new text on Jaron's white board: "Who is she?"

"She is the one who likely retired you both from service. And will perhaps retire me as well."

PROJECT MOLKA: TASK 2
DAY 4 OF 8

 CHAPTER NINE

Molka's eyes opened.

Daylight. In her car. Not moving. Traffic poured by. Where? The Indigo Club parking lot. Dressed. Phone in her jacket pocket. Check it. Day and time: the next day, early afternoon.

Her mind lodged somewhere between confusion and dread. *Something happened to me last night? Something bad?*

She rarely drank coffee, but she decided she needed assistance in pushing logical thought one way or the other. She left the parking lot and found a coffeehouse a few blocks away. She went inside and asked the barista for the strongest thing they had. They gave her something with shots of espresso added to it. She didn't resist when they suggested adding a Blueberry Scone she would never eat. She found a table near the back and sat.

She took a sip. Very strong. The smell of her coffee and of the store reminded her of her Uncle Eli. His home always had a pot brewing. He was a helicopter pilot in the IAF. He crash landed during combat and suffered severe burns to his hands. He was given a medical discharge and got work flying helicopter tours. On her sixteenth birthday—her first birthday living in the foster home and a year before he died—Uncle Eli picked her up and took her to the airport. Her first helicopter ride would be his birthday present to her.

He helped her with the safety straps in the old Bell 407 and they took off. He didn't take her on a touristy sightseeing flight over modern Tel Aviv or the Old City though. He headed straight for the deep Negev Desert. He said nothing while he made hard turns and, low level high-speed runs on the deck, then pulled up and over jagged mountains. These were the same areas he had trained in years before. He proved to himself that day his skills were undiminished by age or injuries.

The pinnacle of the flight was a treacherous weave through the rocky outcrops known as the Amram Pillars.

Molka loved it all. The excitement. The danger. The freedom.

When they returned to the airport Uncle Eli had one more present for her. He took off his military pilot's watch and gave it to her. The crystal still carried a scorch mark from his crash. When she put on the watch she was sure of two things. First: One day, she would fly helicopters in the military too. And the second: This had been the happiest day of her life.

Two years later, on her eighteenth birthday when she left the foster home for military service, her little Janetta told her it was the unhappiest day of her life. Molka told her not to be silly and laughed it off. But she didn't know then what agonizes her now; a life that short shouldn't have any bad days.

Molka took another sip of coffee.

Something happened to me last night? Something bad?
Yes.
Something happened to me last night. Something bad.

She left the coffeehouse, drove to her apartment, and called the animal hospital. She would not be coming in that day. She told them she was sick. Not a lie. She was sick. And woozy. And sluggish. Crippling head and stomach aches. So sick. So woozy. So sluggish.

So sore.

She took a shower. When she finished, she took a second shower. And when she finished that, she got back in the shower, turned on the water, and sat. And waited. And waited. And waited. To be clean again.

While she waited....
Confusion turned to fear.
Fear turned to shame.
Shame turned to tears.
Tears turned to sobs.
Stop it! Stow those tears, soldier! Put them somewhere where they won't affect your mission. You don't have time for crying now. You can cry when you're dead!
Sobs turned to anger.
Anger turned to fury.
Fury turned to decision.
Decision turned to planning.
Planning turned to resolve.
Molka left the shower and searched her closet. What she needed was not there. She got dressed and went shopping.

CHAPTER TEN

"What happened to you last night?" Loto said. "Forgot something, didn't you?" He smiled. "It's still locked in the safe. Come on, I'll get it for you."

9:04PM: Molka found Loto near the front entrance inside The Indigo Club. She wore the results from her earlier shopping trip: a short black leather jacket, black mock turtleneck, tight black jeans, and black tactical boots. Her hair was pulled into a high ponytail with one bang swept across her forehead right to left. It was stylish and practical, keeping her aiming eye clear. Inside her right jacket pocket was the Baby Glock. Inside her left jacket pocket were latex gloves.

Molka followed Loto through the drunks and the dancers to a door marked "Private." Loto unlocked the door and they stepped inside. The club office housed a desk and a large safe at the back. Loto opened the safe, removed the holstered Beretta, and handed it to Molka. She clipped the holster behind her back on her belt.

"You don't have to worry about walking out with it," Loto said. "The owner doesn't work Saturday nights. I'm the commandant in charge."

"Thank you for keeping it for me."

"And thank you again. Turns out that drunk punk with the ankle rig has a felony warrant out of Texas. Shot at some cops. If a guy will shoot at cops, what's shooting a few fat bouncers to him? You gave him a concussion, by the way, which was sweet. Maybe you can teach me that bad-ass kick? Might come in handy sometime."

Molka smiled. "I'm sure you can take care of yourself just fine."

"Didn't see you leave last night though. I guess you went out the private VIP door with the VIPs?"

"Apparently. Is Mr. Sago in the suite again tonight?"

"He was. Him and his little freak friend O'Donnell. Sago left a little while ago. The girls say he goes to the casino when he leaves here. Took the Greek goon with him."

"You mean Maur," Molka said.

"Yeah, Maur. Scary guy, huh?"

"He's intimidating."

Loto waved his hand. "Ah, I'm not afraid of him. I was an All-State nose tackle and All-State wrestler my senior year. Had seventeen full ride scholarship offers. But I hurt my knee in my last match. Couldn't pass a physical. They pulled the offers."

"Unfortunate."

"Yeah, it was. You probably heard about the fight between me and Maur?"

"No, I haven't. Please tell me."

"Sago's your friend; you might not like hearing this."

"We're not exactly friends," Molka said. "We just have business together."

"That's right; you told me. Ok. A few days ago, Sago got that Maur guy his own VIP Suite. Said Maur needed some private playtime. About an hour after he was in there, one of the girls comes running out screaming. Told me he's killing her friend. I run in there and Maur has another girl pinned to the floor with his thumbs pressing into her eyes. She's screaming too. I jumped on his back, got him off her, and almost had him pinned when he started yelling his back was broken. I eased off, but he wasn't hurt. He deked me. Then he did a quick reversal and got me in a chokehold. Turned my lights out. I woke up on the floor with Sago and the club owner standing over me. Sago apologized. He made Maur apologize too. Then Sago tried to give me some cash. I didn't accept the cash or the apologies."

"Nothing was done about him attacking the girl and you?"

"Nothing. The owner asked us to let it go. Personal favor. He said Sago was spending a huge pile of money in the club. So, we let it go. I would love to get another chance at Maur someday though. He choked me out in my own house. Hurt my pride. And if I ever do get another chance, I've got something for his hack moves. Next time, he gets put to sleep."

"You say Maur left with Mr. Sago," Molka said. "Did O'Donnell leave with him as well?"

"No. O'Donnell's still back there in the suite. Partying on Sago's tab again."

Molka wasn't surprised. She knew he would be. The killing luck favored her. She smiled. "Well, it sounds like the work of a bouncer is quite hazardous. I would like to teach you that kick after all. I need to use the ladies' room first. Can you wait here for me?"

Loto sat in the executive chair behind the desk and put his feet up. "Sure. I can do anything I want. Like I said, I'm the boss hoss with the hot sauce here tonight. By the way, I love your accent. It's very sexy. I'm sure your man tells you that all the time, doesn't he?"

"No man."

"Not even a man back home?"

"No man back home either."

"What kind of country are they running over there?"

Molka smiled. "At the moment, I'm happily single and not looking."

"That's what they all say to me."

Molka smiled again. "Just stay put."

Molka stepped back into the club. The DJ blasted a techno set, and the beat shook the air. On stage, the girls danced in fake fog. She crossed the club to the ladies' room. Empty. Like the VIP's VIP Suite, there were no security cameras in there either. She un-holstered her Beretta, released and inspected the magazine, replaced it, chambered a round, and re-holstered it.

Molka left the ladies' room, headed to the door leading to the VIP suites, pushed through it, fast-walked to the hallway end, and applied Loto's "cop knock" on the VIP's VIP Suite door. A sleepy-eyed nude dancer opened and shuffled away. Molka entered and closed the door. The soundproofing swallowed the techno music. She counted eight semi-nude dancers lounging around.

O'Donnell lay on the sofa. He smiled at Molka and said, "What did I tell you, girls? Once you party with Fast Frankie, you can't get enough." He sat up. "Good evening, Molka. I see you've come back to me."

"Yes," Molka said. "I've come back. For you."

"What happened to you last night? You said you had to run out to your car for a second, but you never came back. Did you pass out or something? You were pretty messed up, you know?"

"I don't remember a lot of last night. But what I do remember was pretty messed up."

"Some of the best parties are the ones you *don't* remember."

"Now I'm ready for more."

O'Donnell's eyebrows perked. "Are you?"

"I am. This time my kind of party though."

"What are you saying?"

"I'm saying you and me. Right here. Right now. Alone."

"Serious?"

"Deadly."

O'Donnell smiled and clapped his hands to gain attention. "Ok, that's it for tonight girls. Time to leave. Everyone get out!"

The last dancer gathered her lingerie and exited. Molka locked the door, moved toward O'Donnell, and stopped at an eight-foot distance. "I know what you did to me last night."

"What do you mean?"

"You know."

"I don't think I do."

Molka shook her head in repulsion. "At least let your final act be that of a man. Admit what you did to me."

O'Donnell laughed. "Are you high again? I didn't do anything to you. Like I said, you left here messed up and never came back."

Molka took one step to her left. "Every other woman you've done this to, every woman you've ever abused or raped or worse, is here with us right now. I want you to take a moment and think of them."

O'Donnell's laughing face faded. "You've got no proof and neither did they. The police are funny about these things. They want specific dates and times and places and names. You have any of that?"

"You feel them all here, don't you? Think of them. Think of me."

Just above under his breath O'Donnell said, "The whole time you moaned like a whore."

"What did you say?"

O'Donnell smiled. "I said—the whole time—you moaned—like a WHORE."

Molka's eyes sank to the floor.

"That's right," O'Donnell said. "It's over and done. So, if you don't want to stay and play, you need to leave."

Molka looked up at him. "I'm leaving. But first answer me this: Do you believe in a hell after this life?"

"I don't know. This life is a hell to me. If there is one, it couldn't be much worse. Could it?"

"For your sake, I only hope it is."

Molka pulled her Beretta, assumed a precision Israeli combat stance, and fired six fast rounds center mass into O'Donnell's chest.

O'Donnell folded onto the floor. Molka advanced on his body, firing five more rounds into his back, and the final shot to his head.

She stopped and lingered over her victim.

But now you must learn my ways, Molka. Controlled violence—very useful. Uncontrolled violence—very dangerous."

"Maybe, Azzur. But sometimes also—very satisfying."

Molka re-holstered her weapon and took out and put on the latex gloves. With the sudden stopping of O'Donnell's heart, his front and back wounds only oozed; his shirt containing most of the blood for the moment. She straddled his bloody hair matted head, and searched his body, finding keys, a hotel key card, and a pill bottle in his front pockets. In his back pocket was a wallet. She examined the wallet. It contained several thousand in hundred-dollar bills, a Nevada driver's license, and some credit cards. She put the car keys, key card, pills, and wallet back where she found them. In his left jacket pocket was a capped syringe. She put it in her left jacket pocket. In his right jacket pocket was what she wanted: a cell phone. Unlocked. She scanned it and found her previous night's horror in pics and video. She deleted everything and put the phone in her left jacket pocket too. A deep well on a kibbutz back home would be its fate. Next, she picked up all twelve spent cartridges, zipped them into her right jacket pocket, and sank into a chair.

Molka reached behind her head and tugged on the base of her ponytail.

Unacceptable!

She had defied a key military principle. Allowing a personal matter to intervene with the mission. A personal matter caused by her own carelessness. In the field, you never eat or drink anything you're not one hundred percent sure about. As a result, she had made Sago's longtime friend and trading partner a homicide victim—inside a VIP suite leased in his name, no less. When he found out, at a minimum it would put his guard up. More probably, it would cause his immediate departure for safety in Eastern Europe. Unreachable forever. She detested her failure. She would have to run for home. She wanted a nap.

KNOCK, KNOCK, KNOCK, KNOCK.

Pause

KNOCK, KNOCK, KNOCK, KNOCK.

The cop knock!

Molka vacated the chair and concealed herself behind the bar. She took out the Baby Glock and chambered it.

KNOCK, KNOCK, KNOCK, KNOCK.

Pause

KNOCK, KNOCK, KNOCK, KNOCK.

The door unlocked. Loto entered. Molka stood holding the Glock behind her back.

"Oh hey, you're back here," Loto said. "Sorry to disturb. I like to check on the girls every hour or so to make sure they're—" He spotted O'Donnell's body, walked to it, and said, "Whoa!" trailed by a low whistle. "Looks like you put a full magazine into him. Guess you got into another fight, huh?"

Molka stepped from behind the bar.

Loto turned and observed the Glock in her gloved hand. He put up his hands. "Hey, easy. This guy was no friend of mine. He abused the girls. I hated his guts, actually."

Molka put the Glock back in her pocket. "He raped me last night. I mean he drugged me and took me somewhere and let people rape me. I found this on him." She handed the syringe to Loto.

Loto inspected it. "Probably some kind of GHB. What an enema nozzle. And I made you give up your weapon right before it happened. Damn; I'm so sorry."

"It's my own fault." Molka pulled off the latex gloves. "You were only doing your job."

"After this major fail, I don't think I'll have a job. Oh well. Four years as top man at the top club was a good run. I'll always have a place back in the biker bars."

"I'm sorry. But yesterday you said you owed me a favor. May I ask for that favor now?"

"Depends on the favor," Loto said.

"Wait a few hours to call the police. I can't get a flight back home until the morning. I'll probably be detained before I can leave anyway. It's a small chance though. Could you do that for me?"

"Do I have a choice? Because you're the only one here who's armed."

"I won't force you. As I said, I've done this to myself."

Loto went to the bar, poured a top shelf bourbon shot, and slammed it. He poured another and slammed it too. "Where I come from, to my people, when someone saves your life, it's a sacred thing. I don't just owe you a favor; I owe you all my future days. So, yes, I'll agree to what you asked."

"Thank you. Sorry for the trouble. Goodbye." Molka started to leave.

"But there's a better way to handle this. Better for both of us."

Molka stopped. "How so?"

"What if I told you I didn't want to call the cops? What if I told you there was no reason to call them?"

"I'd still be listening."

"O'Donnell could disappear. He was a multi-decade drug addict. I've known a few. I'm sure he's pissed off and alienated anyone who ever cared about him. He comes here alone. I doubt anyone will miss him anytime soon."

"Except his friend Sago."

"Maybe. But from what I've seen, he doesn't like him much either. I think letting him use his VIP suite was only to sweeten a business deal. Sago usually left as soon as O'Donnell got here."

"How would he disappear?" Molka said.

"I have some friends who can make it happen. They'll want to talk to you first though. They're hard men. Suspicious. They might say no. It's up to you?"

"I'm willing to try."

Loto's eyes went to the ceiling. "Let's see. I've got plastic sheeting and duct tape to wrap him up, so he won't make a mess in the back of my truck. I'll need to get a tarp to cover him. We've got a commercial carpet cleaning machine here to clean up the mess. If I pull my truck into the private lot and take him out the private entrance after everyone leaves tonight, nothing will be on the security cams." He scratched his beard and lowered his eyes on Molka. "It could work."

"Does he have a car here?"

"In the private lot. Looks like a rental. I'll ditch it and torch it over in Tweekerville."

"What's Tweekerville?"

"The bad side of town. The girls told me he scores there, so, he's been seen around that hood. When the cops find what's left of the car, they'll probably figure a dope deal went bad, and somebody capped him and dumped him somewhere. Happens every other day in Tweekerville. That will also give the club some cover. What you would call, uh—"

"Plausible deniability."

"Yeah, exactly. Ok, give me your address and go home. I'll pick you up about noon tomorrow and take you to meet my friends. We got this, Molka. Don't sweat it."

"I admire your confidence." Molka smiled. "Maybe you've done something like this before?"

"As far as anyone knows, I haven't. And that's *my* plausible deniability, and I'm sticking to it.

Yes. She could become friends with this guy.

PROJECT MOLKA: TASK 2
DAY 5 OF 8

CHAPTER ELEVEN

TRESPASSERS WILL BE SHOT!
SURVIVORS WILL BE SHOT AGAIN!
Warned the sign on the front gate.
A sign above that in bold black letters read:
VINDICATORS MC
The clubhouse serving the Vindicators Motorcycle Club sat
on twenty private acres off the Tamiami Trail. The flat roofed
cinderblock structure featured barred windows and a small front
porch. There were about thirty bikes parked in front, all
Harleys—some choppers, some not. Guarding the clubhouse was
a ten-foot-high fence topped with razor-wire and a chained and
padlocked gate.

Loto stopped his truck, with Molka as a passenger, outside
the clubhouse gate and put it in park. He made a cryptic hand
gesture to a guy standing next to the front door who gestured
back.

Loto wore his work attire from the previous night. Dark
crescents under his eyes said he had been too busy to sleep.
Molka wore a pink polo shirt, khaki pants, and tennis shoes. Her
hair was ponytailed and glasses on—a simple veterinarian's day

off style. Her night had also spared her from much sleep. In the truck bed, a large rectangular box sat covered by a blue tarp.

Loto kept looking straight ahead at the clubhouse door. "I've been thinking about this all the way out here. I don't want you to take this the wrong way, and I wasn't going to ask you, but before we go in, I think I better ask you."

"Alright," Molka said.

"When you first came into the club, you said you had business with that Sago guy. Business you felt you needed to be armed for. And I still feel horrible about taking your weapon away from you that night. But before I ask my friends to get involved, can you tell me what kind of business?"

"How much do you need to know?"

"Enough that I know they'll still be my friends after they help us."

"Sensible," Molka said. "I'll tell you what I can." She pivoted in her seat to face Loto. "You have a close family?"

"Big and close."

"And if your family was in trouble, would you be willing to do certain things to help them? Maybe things that weren't exactly legal?"

"Wouldn't hesitate," Loto said.

"Sago has wronged my family. Severely."

"How severely?"

"He took the side of another family who's against us. A family who hates my family. A family sworn to destroy us."

Loto turned his head to Molka. "You mean like a feud?"

"Yes, a feud. A feud which has already cost a lot of blood. My family sent me here to lure Sago to…my elders. They want to talk to him and settle the feud."

"Same way you settled things with O'Donnell?"

"No. They only want to talk to him."

"Yeah ok; I can dig it." Loto punched meaty fist into meaty palm. "Make him see the error of his ways, huh?"

"Something like that. Good enough?"

"Not if I wasn't falling in love with you." Loto laughed. "Joking. Let's do this." He gave another hand gesture to the man by the door. The man came and unlocked and opened the front gate. Loto pulled in and parked. He and Molka followed the man into the clubhouse.

A bar ran along the left wall. A pool table waited in the back. The right wall was covered in motorcycle, military, and sports memorabilia. And up front, seated around a big screen showing NASCAR, sat the South Florida Chapter of the Vindicators MC.

Some sat tall, some stood short. Some fidgeted fat, some lazed skinny. Some wore hats, some wore bandannas, and some were bald. All were embellished with various beard, moustache, and tattoo combinations. Their scent blended charcoal smoke from a grill outside, beer, cigarettes, cannabis, and man sweat.

Molka admired the club colors on their black leather vests. The back patch featured a big warrior-looking guy riding a motorcycle downhill while throwing a lightning bolt. Flames shot from the motorcycle's tail pipes. Located on the vest front were two vertical white patches with black letters. One read VFFV, which Molka guessed was an acronym for Vindicators Forever, Forever Vindicators. But she didn't know what the letters GEOD on the other patch meant.

A member noticed Loto and said, "BABY!"

A collective "BABY!" followed, and all the members rose and hugged Loto in turn. He greeted each by nickname:

Bronco

Waste

Cave Monster

Radical

Sparks

Tombo

Cuda

Yak

Detroit…

A few gave Molka smiling leers, but respect for Loto left it there.

"Damn boy, are you ever going to stop getting bigger?" A stout gray-bearded, and ponytailed member approached Loto.

Loto patted his stomach. "Too much of my mom's Pani Popo."

The two came together in a clamorous, backslapping embrace.

"How is mom?" the member said.

"Good. How are you, Uncle Clint?"

"Good. A little fatter. A little grayer."

"Heard from Bobo?" Loto said.

"He's good. He and his old lady still have their restaurant."

"T.T. feeling better?"

"She's good too," the member said. "Everyone's good. Except for old Mascot there." He pointed to a German Shepherd mix laying in a dog bed next to the bar.

"What's wrong with him?"

"Just old. Probably needs to be put down. But that would break the Brothers' hearts to pieces."

Molka went to the dog and knelt beside him. His tail wagged. She petted him and began to examine him.

"She's a veterinarian," Loto said to the member.

"I was gonna say, she don't look like the stripper trash I usually see you with."

"Molka," Loto said. "This is the legend himself. Clint 'Ramrod' Yates, Chapter President."

Molka stood. "Nice to meet you, Mr. Yates."

"No need to be that polite, Miss Molka. The last person who called me Mr. Yates politely gave me four years state time. Please call me Ramrod."

Molka smiled. "Alright, Ramrod."

Ramrod put a hand on Loto's shoulder. "Now what's this problem you and your friend have that you refused to tell me about on the phone?"

"I refused because I'm not sure who's listening to your phone these days."

"Well, what is it?"

"In my truck."

Back outside, walking past bike-row, Molka admired a motorcycle with a high-gloss black finish. "That's a beautiful Sportster."

"You've got good taste, Miss Molka," Ramrod said. "She's mine. You ride?"

"I have. My ex—I mean a man I used to know—rode. He taught me a little."

"He ride a Sportster too?"

"No, a CBR 600."

"CBR 600?" Ramrod shook his head. "Then you're better off without him."

They arrived at Loto's truck. Loto climbed in the back and removed the tarp and the box to expose the strapped down, plastic and duct tape wrapped, mummy of O'Donnell.

"Oh, that kind of problem," Ramrod said. "That's not a cop, is it? We've got an understanding with law enforcement out here. We pretend we're not doing anything illegal, and they pretend to not see us doing it."

"No cop," Loto said. "Just a drug dealing rapist who got what he deserved. Molka gave it to him. Think you can help us out, Uncle Clint?"

Ramrod motioned for Loto to replace the box and tarp and faced Molka. "Miss Molka, Baby's Uncle Manny, his real uncle, may he rest in peace, my brother, was the greatest man I've ever known. We served in the Marines together, joined this chapter together, and then ran this chapter together for twenty years. And I've known Baby since he was a baby and all his brothers and sisters and cousins too, and there's nothing I wouldn't do for him. And we're all about GEOD. But as to your problem—and this is your problem—I'm inclined to say no. And here are my reasons." He pointed at the body. "I never judge a man on how he makes his living. How could I? He didn't rape anybody I know. And as far as getting what he deserved...well...we're all gonna get that sooner or later. A burden like this you take to your family. And with all respect, Miss Molka, you ain't family."

"I understand," Molka said. "Your reasoning is sound and wise."

POP, POP, POP, POP, POP, POP, POP, POP, POP, POP!

An automatic weapon fired.

Molka dropped and took cover behind the left rear truck tire.

"Nothing to worry about," Ramrod said. "That's just Radical playing with his new toy. You should see him handle this thing. Come on."

Loto and Molka followed Ramrod around the clubhouse to a huge grass backyard. The red-bearded Radical fired a Kalashnikov assault rifle—set on full auto—at watermelons placed atop a row of chest-high posts fifty yards away. He hit and miss—more miss than hit. The members watched.

Molka watched too. Ramrod had made the right decision. Only a fool would let a stranger dump a dead body on them. She hated to ask Loto if he had any more suggestions of where to get rid of her problem. Poor guy. He deserved better. But she must get back to her task. She had already wasted five days.

Focus!

The side distractions and planning on the fly were maddening. In the Unit, mission planning usually took weeks or months. Every detail was covered. Every possibility accounted for. Precision always the watchword. The Major would have chewed her tail rotor off for her sloppiness these last few days. The frustration made her ill, and Radical's poor marksmanship display didn't make her feel any better.

Radical plugged the last watermelon with no shots to spare. "Six up, six dead. Set em' up again, Yak. Now I'm going to show you boys some real shooting!"

Molka had seen enough. "You fired an entire thirty round magazine to hit only six targets?"

Radical looked at her bemused. "These mothers aren't easy to handle, little lady. Especially at that range. Even your average well trained Ruskie soldier will tell you that."

"I can show you a much better way."

"Did you just say you can show me a better way?" Radical and the members laughed.

"No. I said I can show you a MUCH better way."

Radical and the members laughed again. "Have you ever fired an AK-47 before?"

"That's actually a newer model AK-15."

"Ok, have you ever fired an AK-47 or AK-15 or any assault type rifles before?"

Molka crinkled her nose. "A few times."

"Well, be my guest, little lady." Radical locked in another full magazine, handed the weapon to Molka, and joined the other members standing behind her.

Molka waited for Yak to put six fresh watermelons atop the poles and get clear. She clicked the fire selector switch to the semi-auto position, pulled back the bolt, leaned into a combat stance, aimed, and fired. The watermelon left of center disintegrated.

She dropped into a prone position, aimed, and fired. The watermelon right of center disintegrated.

She sprang up, broke to her left at the run for twenty feet, dropped, rolled into a kneeling position, aimed, and fired. The left end watermelon disintegrated.

She sprang up again, broke to her right at the run for forty feet, dropped, rolled into a sitting position, aimed, and fired. The right end watermelon disintegrated.

She stood, walked back to her starting position, lowered the weapon to her hip, and fired twice. The two center most watermelons disintegrated.

Six shots. Six dead.

Astounded silence.

Molka made the weapon safe and handed it back to Radical. "You should lubricate the bolt carrier."

The members WHOOPED AND HOWLED!

Radical got jeered while Molka returned high-fives and answered questions about her moves and firing methods.

Ramrod took Loto aside from the celebration and said, "What in the hell are they teaching in veterinarian school these days?"

"She said she was also in the military in her home country."

"Was in their military or *was* their military?"

Loto smiled. "She's amazing, isn't she?"

"What do you really think about her?"

"And she's really hot, too."

"No, I mean do you trust her?"

"Yeah, I do. I have to, Uncle Clint."

Loto told Ramrod about the skinny drunk with the ankle holster. And about taking away Molka's weapon right before she walked into the O'Donnell nightmare.

Molka joined them. "Thank you for seeing me, Ramrod. Bring Mascot to my hospital tomorrow morning. I can help him. He won't have to be put down any time soon. Now, if you'll excuse me, I need to find a shovel and an isolated piece of ground to use it on."

She headed for the truck, with Loto following her.

"Hold up, Miss Molka," Ramrod said. "I'm going to do something I rarely do: change my mind. Some further information has come to my attention, and I've decided to do Baby a favor. We'll take care of your problem. He'll be gator chow before you get home."

"Thank you," Molka said.

"But one thing. If anyone ever asks you what happened to him, and our club gets mentioned…well, Miss Molka, I'm afraid those gators will get some sweet dessert too."

"Not a problem. I've already stowed all memories of him in the irrelevant bin."

On the way back to Cinnamon Cove, Loto regaled Molka with more bouncer tales. She laughed when he laughed, but she didn't hear them. Her mind was on her task. Sago would soon realize his business associate was missing. What would his reaction be? Call the authorities? Unlikely. Too many questions about O'Donnell's background and the nature of their relationship. Would he get spooked and decide to leave early? Probably at some point—some point very soon.

She couldn't let him get to that point. The next day she would take him.

PROJECT MOLKA: TASK 2
DAY 6 OF 8

CHAPTER TWELVE

Twenty rowdy soldiers surrounded the sand pit. Three bigger muscular soldiers wearing t-shirts stood in the sand pit center, firing each other and themselves up. The surrounding soldiers parted, and a bare-chested giant with a black crewcut and dark eyes stepped into the pit. The three t-shirted soldiers formed a skirmish line across from the giant and taunted him in Greek. The rowdy soldiers laughed. A t-shirted soldier pounced at the giant. The giant's clandestine clothesline ended his surprise attack. Someone blew a whistle, and another t-shirted soldier coiled to advance. The rowdy soldiers cheered. The giant rushed forward and spoiled him with a crushing fist barrage. The last t-shirted soldier slammed into the giant's flank. The rowdy soldiers hoped. The giant wavered but recovered and countered by clubbing him into the sand. The giant bent and grabbed the last t-shirted soldier's neck, picked him up off the sand, and let him hang in the death-vice grip of his hands. The rowdy soldiers pleaded. The last t-shirted soldier's face bloomed purple. His body drooped limp. The rowdy soldiers went silent.

The decade-old video titled, "Greek Giant Destroys Three Soldiers," ended, and Molka laid her phone on the table. If she could find the video online, the associates could find it too.

Which meant Azzur had seen it and didn't feel a need to share it with her. Interesting.

Molka resumed her planning lunch. She sat in the smoker's gazebo outside the animal hospital and fortified herself on protein bars, energy water, and red grapes—her usual pre-mission meal. She worked-out details under headings she had written on a notepad. After watching Maur's sand pit slaughter video, she would have to figure out a safer way to detach him from his master, but otherwise, the main sticking points had all been resolved.

PACKAGE DROP-OFF LOCATION: The contractor team had based themselves in the casino hotel the previous week and scouted the property. Their preferred pick up point for Sago was in one of the casino's four parking garages. She could choose. Give them a minimum eight-minute notification to be in place for her package drop-off. She could handle that.

SAGO'S SURVEILLANCE: Surveillance of Sago in the casino by Corporation employees would not be a problem for her either. They would have to be low key and minimal. Because getting caught there would infuriate the Branch into demanding executive actions. And her presence wouldn't raise any red flags for them. They expected her to come "honey pot" him anyway; Nadia and Warren had told her that to her face. Her not making an appearance would have troubled them more. Once they saw her with Sago, it would confirm their theories, which would relax them and allow their minds to look the other way for a few moments. She hoped.

Finally, her last problem...

INVITATION: *Obtain an invitation to accompany Mr. Sago to the casino, by any means necessary.*

The solution came to her that morning while she treated Mascot for the Vindicators. He had the Canine Parainfluenza Virus, the dreaded kennel cough. She contacted Sago and lied this highly contagious virus was being spread in the area, and as a precaution recommended vaccinating his dogs immediately. He agreed to bring them in the afternoon. When he did, he would either invite her to the casino for the evening or she would invite herself. She wouldn't give him a choice.

Molka was studying a casino property map on her phone when a new silver Mercedes sedan parked in the handicapped space across from her. The car displayed no handicap permit. The driver's door opened. Maur stepped out in a granite colored suit. Why were they an hour early? Maur didn't open the back-passenger door for Sago; he came alone. He identified Molka and stalked toward her.

Molka's mind went to her Beretta. She had brought it to work that morning, but it was inside the hospital, inside the breakroom, locked in a locker, inside her purse, snapped in its holster unchambered, safety on. Military discipline keeping her a neophyte!

Maur stomped up the two steps into the gazebo and encroached over Molka. He held an envelope.

Molka looked up at Maur and smiled. "Good afternoon, Maur. If you've come to be neutered, I'll be very happy to take care of that for you."

Maur stood mute and handed Molka the gold leaf envelope. Her name was embossed on the front and the flap sealed with the initials "GS" in red wax. She broke the seal, opened the envelope, and removed a fine parchment card. A handwritten message was on the card:

To the Beautiful One,

Please come to my home. My children and I are in desperate need of your services and company. Maur shall wait and bring you at your earliest convenience. Please do not leave us long in uncertainty.

Best Regards,
Gaszi

Molka looked back up at Maur. "Mr. Sago has an appointment in one hour. Why can't he bring the dogs here?"

Maur stared at her, mute.

"Does Mr. Sago know we don't make house visits?"

Maur stared at her, mute.

"Is there an emergency with the dogs?"

Maur stared at her, mute.

She knew it was no use because you can't question someone trained not to question orders. But why did Sago want her to come to his house? She knew why: the ancient game of seduction, using his dogs to pick up women. What a pompous creep. She applied the new intel to her plan: go to his home. Treat his children. Accept his appreciation and flattery. Give a little back. Then lock in the casino invite for that night. It still worked. Although, getting in a car alone with Maur was not appealing. She would definitely bring her loaded purse.

"Alright." Molka said. "I'll go. But I need to go get my bag with my examination equipment."

Maur stared at her, mute.

Molka gathered her things, stood, squeezed around Maur, and headed toward the hospital.

Maur followed.

Molka turned around and pointed at him. "No. No follow. You stay, boy. STAY." She smiled. "I mean…just wait here for me."

Located on a barrier island connected to the mainland by two bridges, White Sands Mansion was the largest in Cinnamon Cove, not an insignificant fact. Four floors, 45,000 square feet, done in classic Mediterranean style with cream-colored stucco exterior and a red-tiled roof. Two-hundred and fifty feet of direct ocean frontage offered a magnificent view of the Atlantic washing onto the mansion's private beach. Interior features included eight bedrooms, seven full baths, ten half baths, a grand salon, dual ocean balconies, a massage room, a bowling alley, a home theater, a pub room, a game room, a study, a laundry room, and an eight-car garage.

Gaszi Sago found it reasonably cozy.

Sago's Mercedes, with Molka as the backseat passenger, stopped curbside before the mansion. Maur pointed a small wireless device at the gate, and it began a slow auto-slide open. During the wait Molka noted a pick-up truck parked half a block down the street—twice occupied. A vinyl wrap on the door advertised a generic sounding lawn service name and number. Attached to the truck was a trailer with a large riding mower. The trailer advertised a different name and number, that of a more legitimate sounding rental company. Time costs money when you rent commercial equipment. Maybe if they had unloaded the mower and pretended to be working, Molka wouldn't have identified them as a Corporation surveillance team watching Sago.

Maur pulled the car around the driveway which circled a terraced garden and working fountain. He parked next to stone steps leading to a balustraded porch and the front door.

Molka waited for Maur to open the car door for her, as he had insisted on doing at the hospital; clumsy effort both times. She laughed to herself.

Taking an Intro to Chauffeuring course, Maur? Well, good for you. You're going to need a new career after tonight anyway.

Molka followed Maur up the steps. He opened a massive wooden door and let her pass. She carried both her medical bag and purse, and Maur searched neither. Sago's guard was still down. So far, so lucky.

Molka stepped into a white marble-floored entry hall. Mahogany-railed staircases curved up on each side. Maur chose the left one and climbed. Molka trailed him. The stairs led to a pillared landing which opened on to a large study. Stone fireplaces dominated each end of the room, and plush leather furniture and mahogany tables occupied the middle. Floor-to-ceiling hunter green drapes covered the wall on the far side. Maur flipped a switch, and the drapes parted revealing French doors and windows. Outside them was a stone railed balcony. On the balcony sat a long table with a large chair at each end. The table was set with white cloth and a full dining service. And behind the table stood a smiling Sago.

Maur opened the two French doors and Molka stepped onto the balcony.

"Good afternoon, beautiful one," Sago said. He wore an open-collared white shirt over tan slacks and oxblood leather loafers—a stylish outfit on most other men. He held a glass of red wine. He went on, "I was not sure of your culinary preferences, so I had my chef prepare both a meat and a vegan lunch entrée."

"I'm a rehabilitated vegan," Molka said. "But I understand you asked me here to examine your dogs." Both lay at Sago's feet, happy and panting.

Sago smiled. "I must admit my request was actually a ruse to get you here alone." His smile faded. "Because I know exactly what you did two days ago."

"Two days ago? Let me think."

He knows about O'Donnell!

Molka eased the medical bag off her right shoulder and set it on the deck, leaving her purse on her left shoulder for a cross draw. "I'm sorry. It's been a whirlwind since I arrived in this wonderful land. I can't even remember two days ago, let alone what I did."

"Do not be coy with me," Sago said. "You know exactly to what I am referring."

"I'm sorry, I don't. Maybe you can remind me?"

My back's to the door. To Maur. I need to move!

"Very well. If this is how you wish to play the game." Sago sat in the chair at the far end of the table and lit a scented brown cigarette. "Two days ago—two nights ago, actually—something very unfortunate occurred involving us, more specifically you, at The Indigo Club. This led to tragic consequences. Would you not agree?"

"I guess that's one way of looking at it." Molka crossed the balcony and put her back against the railing.

Sun at back. Better.

Sago exhaled smoke from his nose. "At least you have confessed."

"Have I?"

Someone's coming up the stairs!

Molka's hand went into her purse.

"You have confessed, and now it is obvious what must be done."

"What must be done?"

It's Maur! What's he carrying?

Molka gripped the Beretta.

83

"What must be done is something simple and direct. Something to permanently remedy you from ever again committing such an unforgivable act."

"What would you suggest?" Molka eased the Beretta from the holster.

Sago bolted up and pointed at her. "The next time you wish to see me at The Indigo Club, please inform me in advance. In that way I will not unfortunately be absent, and we will not tragically miss one another." He smiled.

Maur stepped onto the balcony carrying a large silver-covered food tray.

Molka smiled. "I'm afraid you've caught me."

"I understand you missed me by only minutes that night. Fate took a hand. It was not to be."

"Apparently not."

"Therefore, this morning when you suggested you personally vaccinate my children, I recognized you had changed tactics. Instead of coming to find me, you would simply bring me to find you. Correct?"

"You're much too clever for me." Molka pulled her hand from her purse.

"I was flattered by your effort, but I feel this is a much more pleasant setting in which to begin our affair." Sago beamed. "I am so happy you have decided to join the game!"

"So am I, Mr. Sago."

"Please, call me Gaszi. Shall we lunch?"

Molka smiled again. "Yes. I'm suddenly starving."

Maur offered them a choice: mixed grill or creamy garlic pasta with roasted tomatoes. Molka went with the mixed grill to get in her protein quota. Sago went with both choices to get in his calorie quota. For a beverage, Molka opted for water with lemon. Sago continued gulping red wine.

Sago devoured his food without conversation, like a ravenous beast not knowing when it would capture its next meal. Molka mused at his upcoming disappointment. The food in the detention dungeon he would live in wouldn't quite be up to these standards.

Sago finished seconds, lit another cigarette, smiled at Molka, and said, "Was the cuisine to your satisfaction?"

"Delicious. Thank you."

Sago swept his hand toward the ocean below. "And I trust the view is stimulating to your palate as well?"

Molka admired over the balcony rail. Saltwater air carried on a mild Florida spring breeze. Below, a large infinity pool was connected to a raised walkway which ended on a private beach. "It's all stunning. The view. The food. The house."

"Ah, you approve of my humble abode. The resident owners were very reluctant to lease to me. Particularly since this house was not offered for lease in the first place, and with a net worth of several hundred million dollars, they hardly had need of the revenue. However, I found their price and terms were agreed upon."

Molka smiled. "Well, as the old saying goes: you can never be too rich *or* too rich."

Sago laughed. "Delightful! And truer than you know, beautiful one. Truer than you know."

Maur returned and began to clear the dishes. Sago addressed him. "Has Franklin replied to my messages yet?"

"No, sir," Maur said. "Not yet, sir."

"Try to call him again in a few hours."

"Yes sir. Would you like me to go to his hotel and personally deliver your messages, sir?"

"No, let him sleep in peace. This would not be the first time I have known his recovery from weekend activities to linger into a new week."

"Yes, sir."

The monster finally spoke. The subject, and the fact Maur's voice played several octaves above his physique, unsettled Molka. But his conversation with Sago relieved her. Loto was right: O'Donnell's dubious reputation would suppress any concerns about him being unavailable for a day or two. Smart guy, Loto.

Maur left with the dishes, and Sago refocused on Molka. "I apologize for mixing my business with our pleasure. Nevertheless, it is very important I conclude my deal with this man in short order."

"I understand."

"And I understand from my friends at The Indigo Club that you met this same man the other night, Mr. Franklin O'Donnell?"

Molka falsified confusion a moment and said, "Oh yes. I did meet him. Very briefly. When I went to your suite looking for you."

"I hope he did not say anything untoward. He is notorious for boorish behavior with beautiful women."

"Honestly, I'd all but forgotten him."

But thanks for the reminder. Good time for a subject change. Force the issue. Secure the casino invite.

Molka checked her pilot's watch. "Oooo, look at the time. I need to get back to the hospital."

"That is a very interesting patina on your timepiece. Is it vintage?"

"Yes."

Sago held up his wrists. "Do you think it odd that I never wear a watch?"

"Only in the sense that most European men I've seen visiting my country are very well endowed in the watch department."

Sago poured himself another glass of wine and took a slurp. "I grew up in an impoverished neighborhood. It was overrun with violent street gangs. One particularly vicious such gang took a special interest in me—I was a physically weak boy, even for my age. These boys regularly relieved me of my bicycles, pocket money, shoes, and winter coats."

"When I was sixteen, my grandfather passed away and left me a watch that was presented to him upon his retirement. It was a cheap trinket with no real value. However, to me it was priceless, as he chose me, of all his thirteen grandchildren, to have it. I wore it with pride for two days until the boys of this gang took it from me and smashed it under the wheels of a passing streetcar. Simply for their momentary amusement."

"Since that day, I have never worn a watch or any type of jewelry. This is to remind myself that anything of worth can be taken away from you on the simple whim of strangers. Now I ask again, do you think this odd?"

"No." Molka stood, walked to Sago's dogs, and knelt to pet them. "I think everyone deals with a personal loss in their own...unique way. Shall we proceed with the vaccinations?"

Maur held the dogs, and Molka administered the shots. Sago turned away. Both dogs yelped and whimpered. When Molka was finished, Sago hugged them with tears in his eyes.

Molka said, "Thank you for the wonderful lunch. I'll call a ride for myself."

Sago wiped the last tears with his table napkin. "I will have Maur take you back, of course. But we have not yet even talked about your wonderful Haifa. Must you leave so soon?"

"Yes. I need to get back to the hospital. Maybe I'll see you again next week for their check-ups?"

"I am afraid this will be their final check-up before I depart for home."

"Then I suppose this will have to be our goodbye. I hope you enjoy the rest of your stay."

Sago's face fell. "I am devastated that we shall never see one another again." Sago's face rose. "I have just had the most splendid thought. With Mr. Franklin O'Donnell seemingly indisposed this evening, perhaps you will join me in my suite at The Indigo Club for dinner?"

"Well, no offense, Gaszi—"

"She has called me Gaszi! I am winning the game!"

Molka chuckled. "But as I was saying, the...ambiance...you spoke of at the club, is a little too much for me. I wasn't comfortable in that environment."

"Is that a declination?"

"It is. I'm sorry."

"I see." Sago's demeanor portrayed a man seldom refused by a woman to whom he had flaunted his wealth. "Are you familiar with the local casino?"

"I've heard some people at the hospital talk about it. It sounds nice. And fun, from what they've said."

"It is not the Kurhaus of Baden-Baden, but I find it an acceptable diversion. I will be at the blackjack tables after nine. Promise me you will come tonight and be my guest?"

"I will consider," Molka said. "But I can't promise."

Sago smiled. "Well played. And the game continues. Good day, beautiful one."

Back in the driveway, Maur opened the rear passenger door for Molka. She started to get in but backed out. "One minute. I want to get some pictures." Molka took out her encrypted phone. "My sweet Aunt Zillah will never believe I was in such a magnificent house."

Maur stared, irritated. Molka backed down the driveway a few yards to get the colossal mansion in frame. She captured several shots, each with Sago's silver Mercedes in the foreground, including the rear license plate. She would send these images to the contractor team within an hour.

During the fifteen-minute ride back to the hospital, Maur kept a continuous eye on Molka in the rearview mirror. She pretended not to notice, but it disconcerted her and brought her mind back to how she would detach him from Sago in the casino. She had a plan she thought might work, but like she was trained in the Unit, you can always use a force multiplier. The ride offered an opportunity to get one, although it was risky. She would risk it.

Maur pulled up to the hospital front entrance and stopped. He did not move. Instead, he stared at Molka in the rearview mirror again and said, "You may fool Mr. Sago, but you cannot fool me."

"Your master left your muzzle off. How humane. What can't I fool you about?"

"I know what you are planning to do."

Molka's hand went back to her Beretta. "Do you?"

"Yes, and it will not work. Mr. Sago has had much more attractive sleezy women than you try to hustle him."

"That's what you think I'm up to? Hustling him out of some money?"

Maur paused for disrespect. "It is obvious."

"But he didn't tell you that. You figured that out all by yourself, right?"

"I am not the stupid dog you think I am."

Molka bailed out before he could play chauffeur again. She left her purse on the seat and slammed the door. Maur fast reversed, cut a hard turn, and moved toward the exit. Molka waited a moment and sprinted after the car. She came along the driver's side. Maur spotted her and buried the brakes. Molka pointed to the backseat and mouthed "my purse." Maur put the car in park and leaned into the backseat.

Molka opened the door and grabbed her purse. "And I'm not the sleezy woman you think I am." She smiled. "But I can be the forgetful type."

CHAPTER THIRTEEN

"He's losing again," Nadia said. "Unluckiest billionaire I've ever seen. Now he'll chase it all night."

Warren checked his watch: 10:19PM. "Yes, it's going to be another marathon, partner."

Nadia and Warren slouched in rolling office chairs in the Pyanese Indian Reservation Casino video surveillance room. Both wore excellent forged identification badges identifying them as special agents from the National Investigation Branch. The wall before them was covered with flat screen displays linked to the fifteen-hundred plus cameras on casino property. A dozen technicians sat at a console working camera control joysticks and observing. But only a screen located center right interested Nadia and Warren: an overhead view of a roped off single player blackjack table. At the table gambled Gaszi Sago.

"We're in charge of this op," Warren said. "Why do we always pull night strip club and casino watch, anyway?"

"You told me you wanted us on strip club watch."

"That's before I knew you wouldn't allow me to go inside the strip club and watch."

Nadia smirked. "Hilarious."

"Just for fun, let's switch up with Lawn Service tomorrow and take day mansion watch."

"No way."

"Why not?" Warren said.

"For one thing, on mansion watch I can't step out of the truck and relieve myself behind a bush like you."

"You could, you just don't want to."

"I don't want to because I'm not an animal. You animal."

"Biological functions are nothing to be embarrassed about."

"They're nothing to be shared either," Nadia said. "Besides, this mutant theater is a lot more interesting than watching rich people's grass grow."

Warren rubbed his eyes. "If you say so."

Nadia lowered her voice. "And why are you even complaining about domestic duty? Already forgot about our upcoming summer of corporate fun in Khartoum?"

"Ok, I'm shutting up."

"Well, well, look who's come to sweeten our troll." Nadia straightened and pointed to the Sago screen. "I told you this would happen." She giggled. "But it looks even more sad and pathetic than I thought."

Before leaving her apartment, Molka took a final look in the mirror. She wished she could take the red Alexander McQueen dress with her when she left for home the next day; it was tight on the top and stylishly ruffled to above the knee. She chose black heels to match a small black designer purse. Her contacts were in and her hair left down with sexy side swept bangs, right to left to keep her aiming eye unobscured. Just in case.

Molka arrived at the casino at 10:06PM.

Show up late. Make him fear you're not coming. And make him ecstatic and eager to please when you do. The ancient game of seduction.

She bypassed the closer pay parking garages and parked in the free surface lot, as a modest salaried veterinarian would. The lot was almost full, but she found a spot about as far from the casino's entrance as possible. She exited her car. The night matured clear and temperate; it was great flying weather, but this mission, this task, would be all ground based.

The treaties the Pyanese Nation signed did not leave them much acreage, so everything went vertical. They partnered with a major hotel chain whose logo, combined with the Pyanese Nation symbol, glowed neon green atop a thirty-story hotel tower.

Next to the tower, connected by a glass encased walkway, sat the contemporary three-story casino building. The top two floors housed upscale retail and fine dining. The casino occupied the first floor—get them in and get them gambling.

A three-level reserved only parking garage with a private elevator lay under the casino. Using the photos Molka had sent them, the contractor team located Sago's silver Mercedes parked on its third level. Next to his car would be her package drop-off point. The contractor team was already positioned there in a green hotel courtesy van replica.

Molka entered the casino. Ahead, a line waited to pass a security foursome in green jackets. Each carried a hand-held metal detector. "Random" arrivers were stopped, searched, and scanned. An armed officer behind them observed the screenings. She went unmolested and passed a large sign placed for all who entered the casino to read:

Welcome to the Pyanese Nation. Enjoy Your Visit.

It was a busy night with a diverse happy horde on the move. Nice place. Modern décor. Well maintained. The usual casino din of electronic slots. And the usual casino smell of smoking allowed. Molka located the nearest ladies' room and headed toward it. She clipped across a terrazzo foyer, a little unsteady on the high heels. No wonder though. She had spent the last six years in tac-boots, university sandals, and office flats.

The ladies' room featured twenty stalls on one side and mirrors and sinks on the other. There was one visible occupant: a woman reapplying lipstick in a middle mirror. Molka stopped a few sinks away and pretended to fluff her hair. When the woman exited, Molka walked to stall eleven. Its door was locked with an "Out of Order" sign on it. She checked the entrance—no one coming—dropped to the floor, and quick slid under the door into the stall.

Molka knelt. Mounted next to the toilet was a clear plastic two-roll dispenser. One side held a full roll, a white cardboard piece fronted the other side where the roll should be. She reached behind the cardboard and removed an object taped there: a little Colt Mustang XSP semi-automatic pistol. How cute. It came in a composite holster attached to a nylon strap with a Velcro fastener. Nice work. The contractor team was not enthused about her request though. Yes, it was possible, they said. But it wasn't in their contract or even in their equipment inventory. And they could imagine no reason why she needed to be armed. This was only to be a simple package drop-off job by her. True. Then again, they were not the ones who had to detach a 270-pound terrifying brute from the package first. She insisted. They smuggled.

Molka un-holstered the pistol, removed and checked the magazine, replaced it, chambered a round, put on the safety, and re-holstered it. She lifted her dress and strapped the holster high on her bare right thigh. With her dress pulled back down, the weapon was undetectable.

Molka quick slid out under the door. Two tipsy tramps in mini-skirts walking in caught her slide and gave her disgusted sneers.

Molka stood, brushed off her knees, and sneered back. "Oh, like you two have never snuck into a bathroom stall to do something illegal on your knees."

They didn't deny it.

Molka left the ladies' room to take Gaszi Sago's freedom.

"Beautiful one!" Sago said. "You have made me the happiest man in the world!"

"Good evening," Molka said as she arrived at Sago's blackjack table at 10:20PM.

Sago wore another silk Italian suit, brown this time. Maur loomed behind him in his usual blue-grey.

"I feared you would not come," Sago said.

"I almost didn't. But then I thought, why spend another night alone at home?"

"You have made the right choice. And I must say, in your stunning dress, you present a vision of beauty at which Aphrodite herself would weep and tear out her hair in envy. Please sit."

Without prompting, a casino employee brought a chair and placed it next to Sago. Molka sat.

Sago blackjacked the next hand. The dealer passed him thousand-dollar chips in a large stack.

"You see!" Sago said. "You have changed my luck already! And Lady Luck must always be rewarded." He placed the stack before Molka.

"I can't accept that, Gaszi."

"But of course you can. It is nothing. It is yours."

"I'm afraid you don't understand. If I were to accept that, it may seem, it may look, as if I was..."

Sago raised a finger. "Say no more. I do understand and apologize for my crass insensitivity. Years of less than savory female companions have caused my gentlemanly manners to atrophy. It has been far too long since I have enjoyed the company of a fine old-fashioned girl such as yourself."

"Thank you."

"Here is what we shall do. We will donate this to the local animal shelter in your name. Would that be acceptable?"

"It would," Molka said. "And very generous. I hope my luck continues with you."

Sago lost the next three hands.

"Your loveliness has made me bored with this game," Sago said. "And the noise and crowds here make pleasant conversation impossible. Shall we retire to the privacy of my suite at The Indigo Club?"

"I'm sorry, Gaszi. As I said, I'm not comfortable in the gentleman's club environment. Hope you understand."

Sago smiled. "Certainly."

"But maybe...no. Never mind."

"Please tell me your thoughts, beautiful one."

94

"No. I'm embarrassed to even ask."

"Now I must insist you tell me."

"Well, I was just thinking, I enjoyed myself so much at White Sands Mansion today. It's so beautiful, and the surroundings are so peaceful and inspiring. I wouldn't want to give the wrong idea about my intentions though. Would you think less of me if I asked you to take me, I mean, take me to your home?"

Sago took out and lit a brown cigarette. Molka watched him confirm the thoughts she knew he had. Even old-fashioned girls have needs, right? Especially ones a long way from home in the presence of an irresistibly charming billionaire. Azzur was right. Sago's arrogance would be his doom.

Sago blew a deep smoke exhale from his nose and smiled. "Of course, I would not think less of you. Let us go to White Sands Mansion as two fully cognizant mature adults. We will discuss the donation and perhaps some more stimulating subjects. There is no shame in this. Shall we leave now?"

Molka smiled at Sago. "May I have a drink first?"

Sago smiled at Molka. "The High Rollers Lounge awaits us."

Nadia and Warren watched the monitor from the camera pointed at the bar in the High Rollers Lounge.

"Can you believe her dress?" Nadia said.

"What's wrong with it?" Warren said.

"She looks like a hooker."

"Be nice. I think Molka looks like a very sweet young girl."

"Young girl?" Nadia spun her chair towards Warren. "She's older than me."

"Think so?"

"Don't start, Warren."

"I feel sorry for her though. An evening with that disgusting troll. And for what? He won't tell her one thing her people want to know."

"I guess they had to try," Nadia said.

"Whatever he has, they must want really bad."

"No doubt. He's a really bad guy."

Warren frowned. "I kinda wish we could just give him to her. You know, so she won't have to do anything tonight she'll regret later."

"Well, hello, mister voice of the collective conscience. Haven't seen you since Bangkok."

"That was a lost cause. Maybe Molka isn't."

"Who knows? Someday we probably will give him to her, or them. Then later, they'll probably give him back to us. Then they'll want him again." Nadia yawned. "And so on and so on and so on...."

"To answer your question," Sago said after the bartender brought him his second double Macallan. "I have traded in most everything. Soft commodities, hard commodities, futures...these were my education. I made my fortune, if I may be so courageous to say, in shorting currencies. I bet on the failure of others to make my success. However, in recent years, I have moved toward more untraditional commodities."

"Untraditional?" Molka said. "You mean like illegal?"

"Let us call it extra-legal."

"Like what?"

Sago smiled. "Your curiosity amuses me. See if you can guess."

Molka sat up straight on her barstool. "Hmm...let me think. Would that be...um...um...human organs, Gaszi?"

Sago laughed. "You are a delight! I can honestly say I have never considered this. I shall definitely make inquiries though."

Molka took another miniscule Whiskey Sour sip. "How about people?"

"People are a commodity, but trading in them is illegal in most markets. Which makes the risks prohibitive. People are also not as valuable as one would think. The supply is limitless."

"How about information?"

"Ah, now you have hit upon something. Information is truly a commodity worth pursuing. It has become an inconvertible fact in our times: those who control information, control the fate of the world."

Molka smiled. "On that note, are you ready to go?"

Sago commanded the bartender, "Check!"

"Whew." Molka put her hand to her forehead. "I hardly ever drink. I feel a little lightheaded. I don't think I should drive."

"There is no need for you to drive. You will accompany me. My car awaits."

Molka smiled again. "Perfect."

While Sago settled the bill and Maur scouted out their exit path, Molka stood and turned her back to them. She removed her keys, ID card, and both phones from her purse, tucking everything but the encrypted phone into her bra. She turned back to Sago. He offered his arm, she took it, and they headed for the lounge exit.

No one observing from below or above noticed that Molka had left her purse on the barstool.

Nadia and Warren side rolled to the left behind another technician. He monitored Sago and Molka with Maur trailing departing the lounge. The trio weaved through the casino crowd toward the elevator bank near the front entrance.

"She's leaving with him," Warren said. "This is so sad."

Nadia smiled. "Looks like the troll is going to get lucky tonight after all."

The cam tracked the three crossing the terrazzo foyer. They passed a large sign placed for all who entered the casino to read.

Nadia read it too:

Welcome to the Pyanese Nation. Enjoy Your Visit.

"Oh," Nadia said. "Oh no. Oh Shit." Nadia shot to her feet. "OH SHIT NO!" She grabbed Warren's shirt.

"What's wrong?"

Nadia whirled toward a casino security man standing by the door. "GIVE ME YOUR RADIO!"

CHAPTER FOURTEEN

Maur used a keycard to open the private elevator leading to the reserved parking garage. The three entered for the short ride down.

Molka viewed her encrypted phone. "Just want to check my messages. I don't want to be disturbed when we're alone."

Sago smiled. "An excellent idea." He took out his phone too.

Molka sent a two-letter message to the contractor team: PC. Package coming.

The doors opened. They exited into florescent lighting and exhaust fumes. Sago's Mercedes waited in space one, row one, thirty feet away. The green hotel courtesy van replica with the contractor team was backed into the last space at the garage's far end. Molka noted four small antennas mounted on top: a jammer for the security cameras.

Molka stopped and clasped Sago's arm. "Oh no!"

"What is wrong, beautiful one?"

"I left my purse in the bar. On my barstool. It's my Michael Kors. A gift from my sweet Aunt Zillah. I'd die if I lost it!" Molka faced Maur. "Told you I can be the forgetful type. You can move a lot faster than I can in these heels, so be a good boy and go fetch it for me?"

Maur seethed at Molka.

"Do as she asked," Sago said.

Maur gave Sago a concerned frown.

"I will be fine. We will wait for you in the car. Go now."

Maur handed Sago the keys and reentered the elevator.

Molka followed Sago at a slow walk and peered over her shoulder and watched Maur waiting for the elevator doors to close.

Close.

Close!

Please close!

The doors closed.

Security detached.

The contractor team van pulled out and approached at a normal pace.

Sago and Molka reached the Mercedes.

Van forty feet away.

Sago used the key fob to deactivate the alarm.

Van thirty feet away.

Molka observed the van's side door cracked open several inches and that the driver was a female.

Van twenty feet away.

Sago smiled at Molka and opened the rear passenger door for her.

Van ten feet away.

Molka smiled back but did not move.

Van five feet away.

The side door opened full.

Two masked figures prepared to jump out.

Sago bewildered at the sight.

PHOOOOOOM! A violent echo filled the garage.

Molka turned to the source. A metal door at the garage rear had slammed open.

Six green uniformed police officers, weapons drawn, burst out and ran toward them.

The lead officer yelled, "DON'T MOVE, MR. SAGO! DO NOT MOVE!"

Sago froze. So did Molka.

The van's side door closed, and it sped toward the exit.

Four officers ran to Sago. He raised his hands. The other two officers faced Molka—a short female with Jackson on her name badge, and a shorter male with Corporal Ruiz on his name badge.

The four officers with Sago push-carried him toward the back of the garage.

"What did he do?" Molka said. "Where are they taking him?"

"Just one moment, miss," Corporal Ruiz said. "We'll explain everything."

They took Sago through the door from which they had entered and closed it behind them.

Officer Jackson took two steps back, drew her weapon, and leveled it at Molka. "Put your hands up! Do it now!"

Molka assessed the officer's stance and grip as competent. She complied.

"Give me that phone." Corporal Ruiz took Molka's encrypted phone, grabbed her arm, and led her toward the side wall, while Officer Jackson trailed keeping her at gunpoint. On the way, Molka glanced at the exit. The van was gone. Not a surprise. A contractor team would always safeguard themselves from detection first and foremost.

"Put your hands on the wall," Corporal Ruiz said. "Now step back and spread your legs. Spread them farther. Keep your head down, don't look at me."

"And what did I do?" Molka said.

Corporal Ruiz patted her down from the top. He touched her bra, reached in, and removed her other phone, keys, and ID, putting them in his back pocket. He went in for another feel.

"Nothing else in there you can have," Molka said.

He knelt and started to pat up her left thigh, higher, higher, higher…

Molka jerked her head to the right. "Other leg, lover boy."

He moved to her right thigh, patted up, lifted the dress hem, and removed the thigh holster.

Officer Jackson said, "Carrying a concealed weapon on reservation property. That's a big no-no, miss."

Corporal Ruiz cuffed her.

"Where are you taking me?" Molka said.

"Upstairs to the security office."

"And what happens there?"

Officer Jackson holstered her weapon. "You'll be turned over to the sheriff's department and taken to the county jail." She smiled. "The Pyanese Nation is deporting you."

They led Molka through the same door as Sago, up metal stairs, and down a hallway to a small windowless room with a table and four chairs. They sat Molka down, left the room, and locked the door behind them.

Molka's mind caught its breath. She was not certain how what happened had happened. Or why. Or if there was even a small chance left to complete her task and go home. But being arrested and taken to county jail left no chance. That *was* certain. Her fight or flight instinct activated. It would probably take some of both.

Ten minutes later, the door unlocked, and a young man entered. He wore a bright yellow polo shirt with a silver badge pinned to the front and the word "Security" on the back. Around his neck was a lanyard with an ID card and a keycard. He carried some baby fat under a baby face.

Probably a new guy. Good.

The young man placed a large clear ziplocked bag on the table before Molka. "That's your property, miss. It will go with you to the county jail. Your gun is being turned over for state's evidence."

"Where did they take Mr. Sago?" Molka said.

"I think they were just taking him away from you, miss."

"How long will I be here?"

He took a radio from his back pocket, set it on the table, and sat in the chair across from her. "They told me it's probably going to be a little while, miss. It's Spring Break, you know? The sheriff's department is very busy tonight."

"Then any chance of getting these cuffs taken off?"

"I don't think so, miss."

"But they're really hurting my wrists."

"I'm sorry, miss."

Molka smiled and squirmed in her chair to expose more thighs. "Please?"

"You have nice legs, miss. But I'm gay. So…."

Molka leaned forward and read the young man's ID card. "Thomas. Do you go by Tom or Tommy?"

"Thomas."

"Thomas, I'm serious. The officer who cuffed me wasn't professional and nice like you. He was very rude and put them on way too tight."

"You mean Corporal Ruiz. Yeah, he's not a nice man. He teases me about a lot of things."

"Can you please take them off while we wait? It's not like I'm going to knock you out with a quick front kick to the jaw." Molka laughed. "At least not in these heels."

Thomas laughed. "Sure. Why not. They told me to kid glove you, anyway." He stood, went behind Molka, removed the cuffs, and sat back down.

Molka rubbed her wrists. "Thank you, Thomas. Much better. Now I have a question."

"Ok."

"The officers who brought me here wore a different uniform than you and were also armed. But I notice your duty belt is rigged only for handcuffs and pepper spray. Why is that?"

"You were brought here by the Panther Team of the Tribal Police. They handle the most dangerous situations. They're the only ones authorized to carry firearms on the reservation."

"I see. And you're part of a different unit?"

"I'm with casino security. We're called the 'yellow shirts.' We're only allowed to detain people for the real police. We're basically glorified mall cops."

Molka nodded. "Useful information. Thank you."

"I've only worked here a month, but I hope to join the Panther Team someday."

"Good for you. Now please stand up."

"Excuse me?"

Molka stood. "Please stand up."

"Miss, I think you need to please sit back down."

Molka kicked off her heels. "Please stand up, Thomas."

Thomas stood. "Miss, I need you to sit back down please."

"You're a sweet boy, Thomas. I'm truly sorry about this."

"Sorry about what, miss?"

A quick front kick to the jaw knocked him out.

Molka opened the plastic bag, spilled out her things, and stuck them back in her bra. She knelt, rolled sweet boy Thomas over, removed the lanyard from around his neck, and grabbed his radio off the table. She opened the door a crack and peeked out; the hallway was quiet. She closed the door. Obviously, she had to get to her car. But first, she needed to determine her location in the building and pick the least conspicuous way out. She had taken the Survival, Evasion, Resistance, and Escape course a long time ago. What did the manual say? Something about traveling slowly from one concealment point to another.

No time for that. Just get into the clear and outrun or run them over.

The heels would be a hindrance though. She left them behind when she stepped out into the hallway.

Still no one in sight. She soft footed across industrial carpet to an intersecting hallway. To her right, were more doors. To her left, a single door at the end. She went to it, pushed the metal release handle, and eased the door open. Casino clamor blasted her face. She stepped out, joined the mass of patrons, and got her bearings; she was somewhere in the building's back corner. The front entrance was the shortest distance from her car, but not a good idea. She remembered. Evasion 101: Avoid the most obvious routes. Less obvious was a side entrance about 50 yards away. She headed toward it.

The radio in Molka's right hand crackled, and a voice said: "10-98! 10-98! Detainee on the loose. The rookie lost her! The idiot!"

Another voice: "Get off the channel! All officers, this is Director Clemons. We have a 10-98 on a white female, late twenties-early thirties, brown hair, red dress, athletic build. I'm in surveillance. We don't have eyes on her yet. So, Alpha Team cover the exits and elevators. Bravo Team cover the stairwells. Charlie Team cover the skywalk. Let's get her quick before the sheriff's department gets here, because I'll never hear the end of it. And the kid gloves treatment is in effect. Repeat, the kid gloves treatment is in effect."

Molka dipped into another ladies' room to think without cams. Thank goodness for cam free ladies' rooms! The large L-shaped room was busy, but no one seemed to care that she walked barefoot and carried a police radio. The public exits were unusable now; she needed to find a private way out. A small female employee pushing a janitor cart came around the corner, passed by Molka, and exited. A possibility. Molka followed her at a distance.

The radio voice again: "This is Clemons; all teams report."

"Alpha. Nothing yet."

"Charlie. She's not up here."

"Bravo. We haven't seen her."

Molka watched the janitor woman roll to a stop at a door between two slot machine banks and use a keycard to enter. Molka weaved through the human traffic, reached the door, and used Thomas' keycard. It opened onto a long wide service corridor. She entered, and the radio blurted.

"Alpha! Report! Got her! She just went into Mainstreet! Southeast corner!"

Molka ran.

Clemons voice: "Get on her, Alpha. Delta standby, she may be headed your way. And all teams be advised, officer's radio is missing. Switch to alternate emergency channel, immediately."

Molka tossed the now worthless radio into a trash can and blistered down the green and white checkered linoleum floor seeking an outside exit. Startled employees scattered and cursed as she dodged past them.

A side door opened. Two yellow shirt security officers in tandem intercepted Molka as she ran past. There was a three-way collision and fall.

One yellow shirt got up and moved toward Molka. She spun onto her rear end and groin kicked him. He took a knee, gasped, and fought vomit.

The second yellow shirt stood, wobbled, and reached for his radio. Molka popped up and sank him with a roundhouse.

Molka ran on. She approached large double doors with a sign above that read "Receiving."

Maybe a loading dock, a back way out?

She split the doors and ran into a warehouse space with rows of stacked boxes from end to end. A forklift surprise backed from behind a stack in her path. She hurdled the forks before the operator yelled she wasn't allowed back there.

Another yellow shirt appeared on the other side, targeted Molka, lowered his head, and dove at her legs. She side jumped and elbowed his skull in passing. He bit cement and surrendered.

Molka ran again. Still no exits. Only boxes.

Two more yellow shirts came from behind a stack ahead, stopped, and spread their arms. Roadblock. She accelerated and drove a jumping side kick into the bigger one's chest. He fell heavy onto boxes, and heavy boxes fell onto him. She landed on her left foot and spun a hook kick to the other guy's temple. He took a box nap too.

The situation mystified her. What were they doing? Who taught them those tactics? It's like they were trying to corral a runaway kitten. Ok, maybe they weren't trained in martial arts. But they all had pepper spray. Why didn't they use it on her?

Molka trotted onward. She found her exit. There were two big receiving doors located on the back wall—one closed, the other wide open. She blew past more astonished employees, out the door, and onto a raised loading platform, hopping down to feet-cooling concrete. She stood at least a half mile from her car.

A white SUV flashing a blue and red lightbar turned the corner and locked in on her.

That would be Delta Team: parking lot security. Perfect timing. Needed a ride anyway.

Molka put up her hands. The SUV halted to her left. An overweight yellow shirt sloshed out with cuffs at the ready and said, "Place your hands on the vehicle!"

Molka complied. He moved to cuff her. She uncoiled a rear body kick to his paunch. He dry-retched and bent over, semi-breathless. He wouldn't need a side head kick finisher.

Molka jumped into the still running SUV and raced for her car. When she cleared the building corner, another Delta Team SUV crossed her front, stopped, turned around, and fell in behind her.

Real stealthy, soldier. Lead them right to your getaway car.

Molka traversed the huge lot, parked next to her car, and waited. The other SUV pulled in behind. A female yellow shirt got out, young and full sleeve tatted. She came to Molka's tinted driver's window. Molka dropped the window.

The girl's face alarmed. "Oh damn!"

Molka sighed and said, "Here's what's going to happen. That's my car. I'm leaving. You can let me leave or we can do this the other way. Please don't pick the other way."

The girl's nervous voice said, "Get out of the vehicle! You're being detained for the sheriff's department!" She called for back-up on her radio.

"Alright. I like your tats, by the way." Molka opened the door, stepped out, and put the girl to sleep with a humane upper cut.

Molka got into her car and sped for the front exit gate. It was blocked by another SUV. She cut left and raced for the side exit gate. It was blocked by an SUV too.

Trapped.

Maybe not. She recalled a bit of information from the casino property map she had studied at lunch: The Aces High reserve parking garage. It was located in the far back corner and probably used when special events filled the others. Most importantly, it led out to a small rear exit only gate.

Last chance.

Molka tore toward the garage. Ahead, approaching from opposite directions on her flanks, were two more yellow shirts in security golf carts, both positioning themselves to block her from entering the garage.

Don't want to hit them.

But not stopping either.

Going to be close!

Molka punched it and threaded the gap. The carts collided head on, and yellow shirts summersaulted over steering wheels.

Molka's face cringed in the rearview. "Ouch! Sorry guys!"

Another SUV tracked behind Molka. She crashed through the garage entrance gate. The garage was empty. The SUV caught her and bumped her, once, twice, three times, positioning for a pit maneuver. This yellow shirt knew what they were doing.

Better lose them.

She spotted the exit sign on the opposite side and headed for it. The SUV raced ahead and cut her off. She locked the brakes and did a 180. The SUV followed, got on her bumper again, and attempted to pit her again. Nowhere to go but up.

The SUV chased her up a curved ramp.

Level Two.
Level Three.
Level Four.
Molka searched.
Find the down ramp. It leads to the rear exit.
She spotted it, but the SUV raged by her and parked lengthwise to block it.

Molka stopped. The SUV driver watched her and talked into his radio, probably calling more yellow shirts to form a blocking position behind her. There was no going back the way she came.
Treed without a ladder.

Molka had played chicken in a helicopter once—only fun and games. If you didn't pull yours off, you were sure the other one would. Right? Of course they would. But maybe not. Maybe they didn't care anymore. Maybe they wanted to die. Maybe they wanted to take you with them. That uncertainty was terrifying.

Molka stamped the gas and targeted the SUV's driver door.
He didn't move.
Molka kept coming.
He didn't move.
Molka Kept Coming.
He didn't move.
MOLKA KEPT COMING.
He panicked.
He floored it.
He moved.
Molka missed him.

But he had no room to stop. He slammed the side wall with an ugly thud, his radiator exploding into a steam cloud.

Molka stopped, got out, and checked the driver. He slumped into the air bag, unconscious. She raised his head, made sure his airway was unobstructed, and placed her index and middle fingers on his carotid artery. He was breathing and had a strong pulse.

She ran to the side rail and looked down at the rear exit.
Still unguarded. Amazing.
Molka got back in her car and spiraled down the exit ramp.
Level Three.
Level Two.

Level One.

Molka cleared the final curve and smiled.

Made it!

I'm out of here!

No, I'm not!

Molka smashed the brakes. The car side screeched to a stop in a burned rubber haze.

Parked across the exit were two sheriff's cars, lights ablaze with six more lit up sheriff's cars behind them. And behind the cars were ten deputies. Like casino security, they all carried pepper spray. And like casino security, they all chose not to use it. Unlike casino security, they also all carried sidearms. Those they all chose to use, and those they all pointed at Molka.

Molka shut off her car and raised her hands.

CHAPTER FIFTEEN

Over coffee and Black Forest cake, at an umbrellaed table, in a seaside café, on a windswept sunny afternoon, in Caesarea, Israel, Azzur waited for the seemingly gentle old man he called his mentor and chief to finish reading.

"I saved your report on Project Molka for last," the chief said. "Because you ended it with a recommendation for cancellation. A priority cancellation."

"Yes," Azzur said. "Her first task was inconclusive, and she has now failed her second. Failure of a single task is mandatory cancellation."

"I realize this. However, a priority cancellation has never been approved for a project. Or even requested."

"Hopefully this will be the lone exception."

"The difficulty level of the task was extreme," the chief said. "Two previous projects also failed to complete it. Considering this, perhaps she rates some special dispensations?"

Azzur shook his head. "The first two projects—through no fault of their own—were eliminated before ever making contact with the target. Project Molka had the target in hand, and then by a careless error allowed him a literal last second escape. I do not believe in giving dispensations for incompetence."

The chief changed his mind about his last cake bite. "Will you indulge the thoughts of an old retired man? I mean old, formerly retired, man. Excuse my error."

"The only error was your retirement in the first place, chief. At your age, we should all have your strength and energy. And your recall to service was a beacon of hopeful light in these dark times."

"My thanks. But let us talk of you. This past year has been very tumultuous. Our appalling betrayal. The unthinkable losses. The unprecedented reorganization this has necessitated. I am sure being asked to step down as department head and return to field duties was very difficult for you to accept."

"Many others have sacrificed much more," Azzur said. "My personal feelings are insignificant."

"And the difficulty of serving under me again?"

"A privilege."

"Your loyalty is admirable," the chief said, "but not the main reason I originally recommended you as my successor. Nor was the record of your many victories. It was the manner in which you dealt with your defeats, few as they were, that convinced me you were capable of higher responsibility. You quickly abandoned a victory, but you nurtured each defeat. Studied it. Learned from it. Used defeat as a teaching tool, with second chances often given freely to those responsible. Which is why I must now question your reasoning for the quick and permanent dismissal of Project Molka."

"Unfortunate but unavoidable." Azzur took out and lit a cigarette.

"Unavoidable due to what reasons?"

"Her motivation for joining the Program could be troublesome to future operations if she is not under our control. We no longer have the resources to monitor former employees. Priority cancellation is the wise alternative."

The server came by, warmed their coffees, left the check, and smiled away.

"If approved," the chief said, "your request must be handled with the utmost delicacy. She has served the nation with honor. This will be respected. Therefore, it cannot happen here. It would be best done while she is abroad."

"Of course."

"And it should not be contract work. One of our own should see to it."

Azzur nodded. "I agree."

"You have someone in your regular unit qualified?"

"No. My last two are unfit for duty. The rest were lost to the Traitors."

"Who then?"

Azzur puffed and exhaled his cigarette. "I will take care of the cancellation personally. I can leave in the morning."

The chief picked up and looked at the check. "Come to my home for dinner this evening. Hannah will be happy to see you again. Bring the relevant files. After dessert, you will have a decision on Project Molka."

PROJECT MOLKA: TASK 2
DAY 7 OF 8

# CHAPTER SIXTEEN

"**S**tand at ease, Lieutenant," the Major said.

Molka stood at ease before the Major's desk. She wore olive green fatigues with a red beret tucked under her left shoulder epaulette.

"I wanted to say, speaking on behalf of the Colonel and myself, you will be missed by the Unit."

"Thank you, sir." Molka said.

"You are the best pilot we ever served with. You will be replaced, but not really replaced."

"Thank you, sir."

"I understand you plan to pursue a career in veterinary medicine?"

"Yes, sir."

"Very commendable. I'm sure you will be a success."

"Thank you, sir."

"Well, good luck and goodbye."

"Thank you, sir." Molka came to attention and saluted. The Major returned her salute. Molka spun on a boot heel and moved toward the door.

"One more thing, Molka."

Molka turned back to face the Major. "Yes, sir?"

"It's all your fault."

"Sir?"

"You killed her."

"Killed who, sir?"

"Her. You killed HER."

"No, sir."

"YOU crashed the helicopter. YOU KILLED HER."

"I tried to hold it, sir. I couldn't hold it. It was—"

"YOU KILLED HER!"

"No, sir. It was Weizmann who—"

"Sargent Weizmann is a hero! IT'S ALL YOUR FAULT MOLKA! YOU KILLED HER!"

"No, sir."

The Major stood. "IT'S ALL YOUR FAULT MOLKA! YOU KILLED HER!"

The Major transformed into Sargent Weizmann. "IT'S ALL YOUR FAULT MOLKA! YOU KILLED HER!"

Sargent Weizmann transformed into her American Captain. "IT'S ALL YOUR FAULT MOLKA! YOU KILLED HER!"

Her American Captain transformed into a young girl wearing a white dress with pink flowers, a pink bow in her hair, and braces on her teeth. "IT'S ALL YOUR FAULT MOLKA! YOU KILLED ME!"

"WHY DID YOU KILL ME MOLKA?"

"WHY DID YOU KILL ME MOLKA?"

"WHY DID YOU KILL ME MOLKA?"

"Miss Molka!"

Molka opened her eyes.

A large black woman wearing a county jail detention deputy uniform loomed over her bunk. "Wake up, Miss Molka. Your attorney is here for visitation."

Molka rose. "I don't have an attorney."

"Seems you do now. Follow me."

Molka, outfitted in inmate orange and gray rubber sandals over white socks, followed the deputy across the dormitory style housing unit. They passed several inmates seated at a table. A girl said something in Spanish, provoking laughter from the others. Another girl asked where they were taking the princess to.

The wall clock indicated 11:03AM. Molka had tried to nap when she returned from a court hearing earlier, but she had only dozed long enough for a hellish dream.

Near the housing unit front, the deputy unlocked a door, opened it, and flipped on a light. She motioned Molka inside. The tiny room contained a table and two chairs. Another door on the opposite side had an intercom speaker mounted next to it.

"Sit down," the deputy said. Molka sat. "I'm going to strip search you when you're done here, so don't even think about sneaking any contraband into my housing unit. That would ruin my day."

"Ruin it or make it?"

"Don't try me, Miss Molka. You're already in enough trouble. You don't want any more from me."

"No, I don't. Sorry."

The deputy left and locked the door behind her. A moment later, the door across from Molka unlocked and opened.

Nadia entered.

Her blonde hair was bunned, and she styled fashionable glasses with a questionable prescription. She came attired for business in a tight navy blazer over an open-collared white shirt. Below, a matching mini-skirt highlighted long bare legs ending in black heels. She carried a briefcase.

Nadia sat and faced Molka. "How are we feeling today?"

Molka flashed a sarcastic smile. "So much better now. Thanks for coming."

"And how did your hearing go this morning?"

"Wonderful. My bond amount is only slightly more than I made last year. Oh, and I was told when the State of Florida is through with me, immigration enforcement wants me next."

Nadia laughed. "I'll bet they do."

"Are you really an attorney?"

"Today I am."

"Don't I have to sign some sort of agreement in order for you to see me?"

"Today you did."

Molka sat back, folded her arms, frowned, and looked Nadia up and down. "If you're playing an attorney, why are you dressed as a prostitute?"

Nadia's eyebrows popped up in offense. "Funny you should say that, but what do you mean prostitute? I'm wearing a St. John. I got it at Saks."

"In my country, only women of questionable morals and prostitutes dress like that. I wouldn't question your morals, so...."

"And I wouldn't talk, Molka. Passed a mirror lately? Looks like you just walked out of a nightmare."

"Where's handsome Warren?"

"Waiting in the car. You want to fight me again, or do you want to know why I'm here?"

Molka shrugged. "Either one is fine."

"I'll start with some good news. The Pyanese Nation decided not to release any of the security cam video of your great escape attempt."

"Well, there goes my big chance at social media stardom. Why not?"

"They're not required to under their laws," Nadia said. "And it's quite embarrassing to them. You knocked out a big chunk of their security force. They're calling it the worst massacre on Pyanese territory since the Seminoles kicked their ass in 1855." She laughed. "It was very entertaining though. I watched the whole thing."

"Did you? What happened to Sago?"

"They took him back upstairs to the casino, where he gambled the night away and then left."

"Left the country?"

"Not yet." Nadia removed her bogus glasses and laid them on her briefcase. "He's still scheduled for wheels up at 2PM tomorrow."

"So, I have to ask, what did they tell Sago about me?"

"Exactly what I told them to tell him. A bullshit cover story. Just because we burnt you doesn't mean we're trying to burn you. Believe it or not, we're basically on your side. That's why I asked casino security to give you the kid gloves treatment."

"I appreciate that," Molka said. "Now, may I know your lies I'm going to have to deny in court?"

Nadia smiled. "You're a notorious high-class call-girl and drug addict who preys on wealthy men in casinos all over the world. Your method is to lure them into parking garages where your compatriots rob them. You play fellow victim and split the take later."

"Ooo…aren't I the devious little whore? But how did you explain away my very public professional practice?"

"You only became a veterinarian because it gives you access to equestrian tranquilizers."

Molka rested chin on fist. "Why didn't you just give me an incurable venereal disease while you were at it?"

"I did. Hepatitis B."

"Sago's fortunate to have such thoughtful corporate minions looking after him."

"If he only knew," Nadia said. "By the way, the Corporation is now certain you're alone. Which surprises me, because you're not all that good. Overall, the op was well planned. Disrupting the surveillance cams in the parking garage—impressive. We still have trouble with that. And Sago is never without Maur by his side in public. You handled that nicely. But why carry a weapon? You weren't there to kill them. Huge and obvious mistake. All it could do is get someone hurt. Or get you caught."

"How did they know I was armed?"

"I told them."

"And how did you know?"

"Because anyone trying to take something away from Maur damn well better be. But honestly, it was more of a lucky guess. One of my talents. Luckier than usual though. Them putting you in here and out of our way is like winning a mini vacation. I should thank you, but mistakes like you made are painful to me. Especially when made by my adversaries. Cheapens my success. Like I'm only up against a…"

"Neophyte?" Molka said.

"Good word for it. You know, *ketzelah*, taking pride in your craft can go a long way toward being good at it."

Molka's face turned irritated. "Being good at it? You think that's what I want? I'll tell you what I want: I want nothing more than to be back in my little country in my little office with my little animals. And all the big bad Corporations and big bad Sago's, and with all due respect, big bad Nadia's of the world, can go find the nearest hell hole and fall into it."

"Then why did you take the job?"

"It doesn't matter anymore." Molka leaned forward and laid her head cheek down on the table. "I wish I could take a nap."

"Ok. I'll leave and let you get to it." Nadia started to stand.

"I was in the military," Molka said. "A helicopter pilot with special forces. My unit was sent to eliminate the leadership of an extremist group—I won't say which group or in which country—who kidnapped and executed two of our soldiers. The mission was successful. At least we thought at the time it was. On the way out, we took ground fire from surviving members of this group. My helicopter was hit several times. One of the hits—a lucky shot, really—caused a sudden hydraulics failure. No chance I could get us back into friendly territory. I brought us down with a controlled crash. Everyone survived."

"While we waited for another helicopter to extract us, we we're assaulted by at least twenty-five militants. We engaged them in a firefight. Two members of our team were wounded. The rescue helicopter arrived. It was going to be close. The enemy closed to within twelve meters of our perimeter. One of our team members, Sergeant Weizmann, removed a door gun on the helicopter and charged them. They ran. The rest of us got on board. Sergeant Weizmann ran to join us and got hit. We saw him go down. It looked fatal. They were right behind him and started firing at us again. We barely got out. Another team came back for Sergeant Weizmann's remains later, but his body was gone. We thought locals buried him."

Molka raised her head. "We found out later the leadership of the extremist group wasn't there during our mission. But some of their family members were. An explosive charge used to open a reinforced door killed an eight-year-old boy, the son of one of the leaders. We took this hard. We were told there would be no non-combatants present."

"We also learned Sergeant Weizmann didn't die that night. The extremist group carried him off, got him medical care, and saved his life. When he was well enough to talk, they tortured him. Sergeant Weizmann was strong and brave and stood up to it for days, but in the end, like everyone under professional torture, he broke. They videoed parts of his torture and his execution. They sent our government the tape. I heard it's unwatchable."

"A year to the day after that mission, six simultaneous explosions went off in my country. Each one killed a family member from my team of that night. It was later revealed, while under torture, Sergeant Weizmann had given the extremists some of our names."

A single tear escaped each of Molka's eyes and crawled down her cheeks, but her voice remained strong. "One of the explosions, a car bomb, killed my eleven-year-old sister Janetta. It also killed the foster parents she lived with at the time. I never got to meet them. They were taking her to the first day at her new school. I should have been there for that. She sent me a picture of herself in the outfit she would wear. It was a white dress with pink flowers on it. She wore a pink bow in her hair. She was smiling. She had just got braces put on her teeth. I still have the picture. It's on my desk in my office. I eat lunch with her every day."

"So, you asked why did I take this job? The person, the thing, the one who took away my little Janetta still lives. And so do I. And I can't live with that."

Nadia rubbed her eyes and put the fake glasses back on. Behind them her eyes glistened moist and red.

"I've never told anyone that before," Molka said. "Not sure why I told you. I'm not sure about a lot of things anymore. Except I've let her down again."

Nadia stood, picked up her briefcase, pressed the intercom button next to the door she had entered from, and said, "I'm ready to leave." She turned back to Molka. "The Corporation contacted the state attorney's office and the Pyanese Nation. Tomorrow afternoon, when Sago has left the United States, all charges against you will be dropped and you'll be released."

A deputy unlocked and opened the door for Nadia. Before stepping out she said, "You know, I also… What I mean is…I hope someday…you find what you're looking for."

"Miss Molka!"

Molka opened her eyes. It was after midnight and she had yet to sleep. Another large female deputy loomed over her bunk. "Wake up, Miss Molka. Your bondsman is here."

Molka rose. "I don't have a bondsman."

"Seems you do now. Follow me."

PROJECT MOLKA: TASK 2
DAY 8 OF 8

CHAPTER SEVENTEEN

An impassable door opened. Molka stepped through, freed into the county jail's front lobby. She was redressed in her dress from two nights earlier, which was worse for the wear with fight and flight wrinkles. She carried a plastic bag with her phones, ID, and keys. She didn't leave barefoot though. The male employee who returned her property broke policy and allowed her to keep her jail sandals, the type of allowance beautiful women get from men at 2AM.

Molka identified her probable "bondsman" in the lobby seating area. He entertained two recently released working girls. She waited behind him while he finished his story.

"So, another time, this guy comes into the club and tells me he's a professional gambler. And I say, well I'll *bet* you'll have fun here tonight. Ha ha ha. But he doesn't laugh. He says, 'You don't understand. I'm so compulsive now I must put myself in physical danger to be satisfied.' Then he took out a hundred-dollar bill, spit on it, wadded it up, bounced it off my forehead, and said, 'I'll bet you a thousand you'll pick that up.' I didn't pick it up. I escorted him out. When we get outside, he spits on another hundred-dollar bill, bounces it off my forehead again, and says, 'double or nothing?' And again, I didn't pick it up. I explained to him that the root cause of most addictions is unresolved trauma. The function of the addiction is to divert these painful feelings into a seemingly comfortable alternative without allowing them to become conscious. But if you're brave enough to face these feelings, and resolve them in a positive way, the psychological grip of an addiction can disappear very quickly."

"Great advice," one girl said.

The other girl said, "Then you playfully wished him *good luck* on his recovery and said goodbye?"

"No. Then I knocked his dick in the dirt, put boots to him, and waited for the manager to call the paramedics. Damn dumb-ass professional gamblers. But I shouldn't say that. I'm sure most professional gamblers are fine people. And I try to love everyone. I'm just a humble man of peace."

"And are you also a bondsman?" Molka said.

Loto turned around. "Nope. I paid straight cash for you."

"Then you're also my hero. Thank you."

"Don't thank me yet."

Outside in Loto's truck, he said, "You believe both those girls gave me their numbers?"

Molka said, "Maybe not the take-home-to-meet-your-mother kind of girls though."

"Hey, don't hate. One of the finest girls I know was recently in jail."

Molka removed her things from the plastic bag. "Better stay away from her kind too."

"Tough for me. I've always been a sucker for a bad-ass chick. But those two probably just want jobs at the club."

"How did you know I was here?"

"People come tell me things. Guess you want to go home now?"

Molka checked her encrypted phone. Dead. "Yes. Going home is all that's left for me to do."

"Ok, I'll drop you off. But first, I've got a few get out of jail surprises for you."

Loto reached behind the seat, retrieved a gym bag, unzipped it, and removed a leather Vindicators' vest with a lone patch on the back that read "Prospect."

"The Brothers wanted you to have that with their thanks," Loto said. "Whatever meds you gave to old Mascot have him up and running around like a pup again. Made some grown men cry. It's just honorary, but you're the first female they've ever given prospect status to."

"I'm flattered."

"Ramrod also said to tell you taking care of O'Donnell was a favor to me. They still owe you one for Mascot."

"I'm glad Mascot feels better."

"And here; this is from me." Loto reached into the bag again and took out a braided rope cord necklace. From it hung a three-inch by one-inch carved wood flower painted a vibrant red.

"It's beautiful. What kind of flower is this?"

"The Teuila. National flower of Samoa. They make these necklaces in my family's native village. My Uncle Manny gave it to me. Supposed to bring good luck."

"Good luck was something I desperately needed. But I can't accept this. It's personal to you."

"That's why I want you to have it."

Molka took the necklace and put it on. "Then I'll wear this with pride."

"There's a little more to it. Pull on the stem at the bottom of the flower."

Molka grabbed the stem and pulled. A little dagger slid out from the flower's body.

"Cute. Beautiful with a deadly surprise."

Loto smiled. "Just like you. But you caught a weapons charge. You're probably going to lose your CW license. At least for a while. So, I figured if some undesirable enema nozzle got too close again, you could give him the surprise of his life with that."

Molka noted the blade's sharpness. "I see what you mean. By the time he figures out what's happening to him, it's too late. It's already happened."

"You got it."

Molka re-sheathed the dagger. "Thanks again for getting me out. I have some money, but I can never fully pay you back."

"You don't have to pay me back. That's the other surprise. Your aunt gave me the cash."

"My aunt?"

"Yeah. Your Aunt Zillah. She came in the club last night."

"You met my sweet Aunt Zillah? She didn't need a shave, did she?"

"No. She was sweet, like you say. Told me what happened to you. Asked me if I would go bail you out. Carried the cash with her in a big purse. Said she flew all night from Vancouver, Canada to get here. She wanted to come herself, but said she had an important task to finish and had to fly straight back. Said you would understand. Made this little video for you though." Loto took his phone from his pocket, opened a video, and handed the phone to Molka.

On screen, a sweet looking woman in her seventies stood outside The Indigo Club. She took a document from her pocket and read it aloud in Israeli Hebrew.

"Molka, this is your Aunt Zillah. I was very distressed to hear of your recent difficulties. Against the advice of some in our family, it has been decided to give you this opportunity to redeem yourself. You have one day to make amends. All family associates are still available to you. Understand, dishonoring the family again will not be tolerated."

The video ended. Molka's eyes left the truck's interior darkness and focused on the brightly lit parking lot. Apparently Azzur was monitoring her. How typical of him. And apparently Azzur had talked the Counsel into giving her another chance. How atypical of him. But he had selfish reasons. She was his project. Her failure had to be as embarrassing to him as it was to her. Maybe more so—right? But the reasons didn't matter. She knew what she would do and how she would do it. It came to her in an instant of lost clarity recovered. Everything she needed was right there, even offered to her. It might work. It could work. It must work. Another chance. Another chance for her little Janetta. She suppressed new tears.

Molka turned her head back and handed the phone to Loto.

"Hey, you're upset," Loto said. "You must really miss your aunt?"

"What? Yes. Do you know where they took my car?"

"It will be over in the county impound lot."

"Can you take me to it?"

126

Loto nodded. "I'll run you out there later today after I wake up. How about around noon?"

"How about right now."

"Ok with me. But is everything ok with you? I saw this same look on your face right before you wasted O'Donnell."

"What would you think if I told you I could get you another shot at Maur?"

"I would think you and your…elders…haven't given up on straightening out that Sago guy."

"We haven't," Molka said. "But it must be today. He's leaving the country this afternoon."

Loto scratched his beard. "Maybe he is. Maybe he isn't."

"I like your attitude." Molka plugged her encrypted phone into Loto's charger. "Two more questions. One, ever heard of White Sands Mansion?"

"Everyone around here has. Why?"

"I'll tell you on the way to get my car. Let's go. And go fast."

"Right." Loto started his truck and sped toward the exit. "What's the second question?"

"What time do the Vindicators usually wake up?"

 CHAPTER EIGHTEEN

"Welcome to Miami."

"Are we alone?" Azzur said.

"Yes. I sent my gunsmith to lunch early, as you requested."

"Where is it?"

"Here under the counter." He smiled. "I want to thank you for giving me this opportunity."

"Lock the door and put up your closed sign."

Azzur removed his leather jacket and watched the namesake owner of Kaufmann Firearms obey him.

The short 60-ish man with thick white hair and eyebrows popped a new smile on his way back to the counter. He opened a lower drawer, removed a small black semi-automatic pistol and a suppressor, and laid them side by side on the glass top. "Here you are: Beretta Model 71. A real classic. Haven't seen one of these in a long time."

"Where did you obtain it?"

"A dealer in Lexington, Kentucky."

"And the suppressor?"

"My own design," Kaufmann said. "To your specifications."

Azzur picked up the pistol and smelled the barrel. "You have tested it?"

"Yes. I put 75 rounds through it, replaced the recoil spring, cleaned and lubricated it. The weapon is in excellent working condition."

"Ammunition."

Kaufmann turned, removed a 50-round box of .22LR from a shelf, and placed it next to the pistol.

"One magazine will be sufficient." Azzur handed him the pistol. "Load it."

Kaufmann removed the magazine, opened the ammo box, and began to load it. "These pistols are legendary. Quite a fascinating history, to say the least." He smiled again. "Allegedly, once the preferred weapon of our assassins."

Azzur took a packet of cash from his pants pocket. "How much?"

"No charge, of course. I'm happy to do my part." Kaufmann refreshed his smile. "But should I watch the local news for the next couple of days with personal interest?"

Azzur took the magazine from Kaufmann and finished loading it. "You live at 9653 Floriway Avenue."

"Yes, how did you—"

"Your wife is very beautiful. Maybe a little young for you, I think."

Kaufmann's smile dissolved. "We met through a mutual friend. She was—"

"Does she lay out by the pool every day in the very tiny pink bikini?"

"Were you at my home?"

Azzur picked up the pistol and inserted the magazine.

"Did you see my wife?"

Azzur screwed on the suppressor.

"Did you talk to my wife?"

Azzur chambered a round.

"I asked if you talked to my—"

Azzur pointed the pistol at a promotional poster over Kaufmann's shoulder.

Kaufmann eased his hands palms down on the counter. "I just wanted to...I didn't mean anything. Please. Don't think that I would ever...I'm sorry if I've offended you. I don't want any trouble."

Azzur tucked the pistol inside his waistband and tossed the money packet on the counter. "Neither do I."

CHAPTER NINETEEN

"**B**ronco's Mile High Mowing - Grass and Weed Specialists."
The driver in the fake lawn service truck parked half a block
down the street from White Sands Mansion used binoculars to
confirm it. "Yep. That's what the sign says alright."

"Figures," the passenger in the fake lawn service truck said.
"Only two hours left on a three-week job and the real lawn guys
show up."

The two fake lawn service men watched the older black van,
with its crude white business sign taped to the side, parked at the
curb outside the mansion's front gate.

"I was afraid of this," the driver said.

"Call it in?"

"You want to bother the blond beast on her day off?"

"No, I do not," the passenger said.

"They're getting out," the driver said. "They made us. Here
they come." He lowered the binoculars. "Play stupid."

Two long-haired men in t-shirts, jeans, and bandanas crossed
the street. They split and approached the fake lawn service truck
from both sides.

Vindicator member Bronco stepped up to the driver's door. "What the hell you boys doing sniffing around our block? We've got every blade of grass you see under contract."

"We're totally lost," the driver said. "Looking for Palmetto Place Manor. But all these big castles look the same. Maybe you guys can help us?"

"We can't help you," Vindicator member Detroit said from outside the passenger's window, "but you're about to help us."

The driver started to answer, but Molka's car pulling up to the mansion's front gate stifled him. They watched her exit her car, stride up to the gate, and press the call button. The driver and passenger silently panicked, glancing at each other and then back at Molka.

"If I were you, I wouldn't worry about her," Bronco said, pointing at Detroit. "I'd worry about him."

Detroit aimed a Ruger .45 at their heads.

"Put your hands on the dash and stay still," Bronco said, "and I'll take the phone you're trying to hide under your ass cheek there." He reached in and took the phone.

The driver said, "You guys take the lawn service business really serious. We'll move along. Hey, like you said, it's your block."

"Cut the horseshit, sugar tits," Bronco said. "You know we're not out here to mow any lawns either."

"We're just working men," the driver said. "We don't have much. But you can take what we have."

"We're not going to take anything from you," Detroit said. "We're going to give you something."

"What's that?" the passenger said.

Bronco smiled. "Your choice. You can have a couple of hot bullets out here, or a couple of cold beers in our van."

The driver smiled. "We'll take the beers."

 CHAPTER TWENTY

"I see they've let the whore out of jail," Maur said.

"And I hear the master has taken the muzzle off the dog again," Molka said.

At 12:03 PM, on an unblemished spring south Florida day, Molka stood outside the White Sands Mansion front gate, talking into a speaker and looking into a security camera.

She wore a knee-length white sun dress with red floral print, the best thing in her closet to say, "I'm not the prostitute they told you I am." She accessorized the dress with a matching necklace—Loto's lethal good luck charm—and her pilot's watch. Her hair was styled in a high ponytail with bangs swept across her forehead right to left, to clear her aiming eye. No more high heels to be worn on ops; so, if asked, she would explain that her black tac-boots were the latest trend in SoBe.

In her car was a large shoulder bag containing both her phones and both her weapons.

"Mr. Sago does not wish to see you," Maur's speaker voice said. "Mr. Sago wishes you to leave these premises at once."

"Tell him I want to apologize for the misunderstanding the other night."

"Mr. Sago wishes you to leave these premises at once."

"Tell him I also have information. Information to trade."

There was a thirty-second pause, and then Sago's voice, "What information do you have to trade?"

"I know the whereabouts of Frank O'Donnell."

The front gate auto-unlocked and began its slow slide open. Molka got back in her car to wait and reassess the operation.

Bronco and Detroit had neutralized the Corporation surveillance team watching Sago, and her entry ploy had worked. *Good start.*

But having her diversion "team" jump off from her apartment, a twenty-minute ride away, troubled her. It couldn't be helped though. Staging an outlaw motorcycle club in or near the multi-millionaire neighborhood would be, as the Major used to say, as conspicuous as a drunken brown bear in a rented white tux.

The contractor team waited in the casino hotel. Molka's request that they meet her outside Sago's home for delivery was denied. Sago must be turned over to them on Pyanese Nation territory. No exceptions. Apparently, plausible deniability outweighed practicality or safety or sanity. But they had an idea. They told her to incapacitate Sago and drive him in his own vehicle to the lesser-used side hotel entrance. Waiting there would be a female "hooker" with a wheelchair. The hooker would put Sago in the chair and wheel him inside. Three uniformed "Tribal Police officers" would immediately intercept them. And once again, they would take Sago into protective custody for his own safety from a notorious hooker's criminal schemes. This time he would be hustled away in a "Tribal Police van." The hooker too. All played out live on casino security cams. She had to admit, it was a nice improvisation for simple package processors.

She would then leave the Pyanese Nation in Sago's car and ditch and clean it in an appropriate manner—a Loto-style torch job.

And as for Loto, he got the most dangerous assignment. She told him he was the key to the operation. If he accomplished his objective, there was a chance everyone would leave alive. If he failed, someone would probably have to die. He accepted the challenge without fear.

The gate opened. Molka drove through and parked behind Sago's silver Mercedes in the circular drive. She grabbed her bag and cat footed up the stone porch steps. The front door waited open. She looked inside. No one. She tiptoed into the marble entry hall. Sago's scented brown cigarette waft announced his presence, but there was no stench of the Maur threat.

Where is he?

Stacked against the wall near the door was an expensive custom luggage set. Sago was preparing to leave soon. But not where he thought. Molka took out her regular phone and messaged Loto: "GO."

"Come join me, Molka," Sago's voice said from the upstairs study. "Let us find out what you know."

Molka climbed the curved staircase. She reached into her bag and gripped the Beretta.

Where's Maur?

She stopped next to a large pillar atop the stairs. Across the room, Sago wore a black silk robe over white silk pajama pants and smoked on a sofa. Both his dogs sat beside him. They wagged their tails and jumped down to jump on and greet Molka.

Molka returned the greeting. "Where's your other dog?"

Sago smiled. "You will see him imminently."

And Molka thought she did.

For half an instant.

When he stepped from behind the pillar.

And just before his brick-fist connected with her chin and made the world dark.

CHAPTER TWENTY-ONE

"**A**nything yet?" Ramrod said.

Loto checked his phone and shook his head. "They've only been gone twenty-two minutes though."

Ramrod, Loto, and Radical sat at the small table in the pass-through kitchen of Molka's apartment. Sitting and standing around the living room were the twenty most trusted members of Vindicators MC.

"Ok," Ramrod said, "let's go through it again."

"Again?" Waste said. "We've went through it three times since they left."

"And we'll go through it three more times, and three more times after that, until you can puke, piss, and poop it."

"That's the old Marine in him talking," Loto said.

"Damn right it is. Cuda, you tell it."

Cuda swallowed his latest longneck beer pull. "We're gonna ride over to some rich asshole's house on the island. Sparks is going to pop the gate, and we're gonna go in and re-landscape his yard. And when the rich asshole comes out to yell at us, Baby's gonna slip in the back, find this rich asshole's big ugly friend and kick his ass. And while he's doing that, Molka's going to grab this rich asshole and take him to meet her people."

"And?" Ramrod said.

"And she said she's gonna have to knock this rich asshole out, and he's a fatass, so she might need help getting him in the car. Me and Yak will take care of that. And then we're all gonna escort her to the casino and make sure no one follows her."

"Why does it have to be the casino?" Cave Monster said.

"I asked her the same thing this morning," Loto said. "She said her people are staying in the hotel there."

"We need to be in and out, five minutes max," Ramrod said. "So, Sparks, I don't want you fiddle farting around with the front gate. I want it open in under five seconds."

"Not a problem," Sparks said. "I brought bolt cutters and a sledge. And if they don't get it done, this will." He pulled a .357 from behind his back.

"No weapons," Ramrod said. "Molka was clear on that. Like she said, we're not going there to kill them, and we don't want to get anyone accidently hurt."

Sparks frowned disapproval. "You let Detroit leave here strapped."

"Just for prop purposes," Ramrod said. "It's not loaded. Leave your weapons here if you brought one. Everyone got that?"

"Got it."

"Ok."

"Yeah."

"If I have to."

"Before we do this," Radical said, "let me say something. First, I don't mind helping her out. Like you say, she saved Baby's ass. And Mascot too. We owe her one. And it was complaints by those rich assholes living on the island that got us run out of Cinnamon Cove. Remember?"

"Damn right"

"Yeah, they did."

"Still pissed."

"Snobby sons of bitches."

Radical went on. "But isn't anyone else even a little worried about the planner?"

"What do you mean?' Ramrod said.

Yak said, "He means he thinks he could've come up with a better plan."

Ramrod said, "I know you're bucking for the Sergeant of Arms stripes when Bronco steps down. But just the way she punked you out with your own AK makes her look like a regular George S.—by-God—Patton compared to you!"

The members laughed.

"That's not what I mean," Radical said.

"Then what the hell do you mean?"

Radical spread his arms. "I mean look at this place. Neat, organized, the home of a total professional. And when we took Mascot to see her at the hospital, she was knowledgeable, efficient, a total professional. Even when she was punking me out, she was smooth, cool, and a total professional. But did you notice her today when she told us her plan? She had a wild desperate look in her eyes and fear in her voice. She tried to keep it in check, but you could see it and hear it."

"I noticed that too," Ramrod said.

"Molka's ok," Loto said. "I've got good feelings about her."

"You've known her for a few days," Radical said. "You really don't know anything about her."

"I know she saved me and my guys from bullets. And that's all I need to know."

Cave Monster laughed. "Baby's letting his little head rule his big head again."

Loto said, "Yes, Molka was a little stressed. She also told us she's never done anything quite like this before. But she's a bad-ass. She can do it. Give her plan a chance."

"A chance?" Radical said. "We're riding in behind her blind on a chance? A lot of good armies have been lost to chancy half-assed planning." He stood. "I say we abort this abortion of a mission before it's too late. Who's with me on this?"

"For once, I might agree with Rad."

"Minding my own business has always worked best for me."

"I go to jail again, my old lady's gone."

"Mine too."

Loto stood. "You know, I hate to say this, but I'm actually glad my Uncle Manny's dead right now. Because if he had lived to see Vindicators act like this, like scared little whiny punks, he'd of…. Never mind. If you guys want to back out, go ahead and back the hell out. But I'm still going. Sparks, give me those bolt cutters."

Ramrod stood. "The next time we back out of something will be the first time! I gave Miss Molka our word. So, ain't nobody backing out of nothing. Right?"

The members went silent.

"I said, RIGHT?"

"Rad's just talking trash as usual."

"My friend's troubles have always been my troubles too."

"Jail chow's better than my old lady's cooking anyway."

"Mine too."

"Damn straight," Ramrod said. "Let's go through it again. Tombo, now you tell it."

Loto's phone notification sounded. He read the message. "GO code! She's in!"

"Mount up, Vindicators," Ramrod said. "Let's go GEOD."

# CHAPTER TWENTY-TWO

I'M DROWNING!

I'M DROWNING!
I'M DROWNING!
I'M DROWNING!
"I'M DROWNING!"

Maur stopped pouring water from a large pitcher onto the rag covering Molka's face. Her hair and dress top were soaked.

"You're not drowning, whore," Maur said. "You only feel the sensation of drowning. I could do this to you for hours, for days, and you would never die. You would just wish to die. Horrifying, isn't it?" He poured more water on her face.

When Maur slapped Molka awake ten minutes before, she found herself in the mansion's laundry room strapped atop a table. He towered over her, shirtless. Up close, his massive musculature appeared freakish. She didn't tell him about her drowning fear. But once he started the waterboarding torture, he sensed it and exploited it. After five minutes, she answered all the questions Sago asked her. She had no choice.

Maur stopped pouring and removed the rag.

Molka coughed and gasped, "You're drowning me! Please don't drown me! I've told him everything he asked. Kill me, but please don't drown me."

Maur smiled, put the rag back over her face, and started to pour again.

"I believe that will be enough," Sago said from the corner.

Maur stopped and removed the rag.

Molka coughed again. "Thank you. Thank you."

Maur set aside the pitcher and left the room.

"I truly regret it came to this, beautiful one," Sago said. "But you must understand, when you said you knew the whereabouts of Franklin O'Donnell, it was imperative I found out you told the truth." He crossed the room and came to her side. "I was under the assumption you were a drug addict, and drug addicts have a propensity to lie. Your reason for killing him was perfectly valid. Nevertheless, in doing so you also nullified our deal. This will cost me not an unsubstantial sum. However, good fortune in business has always favored me." He lit a brown cigarette, and his nose exhaled smoke above her. "Your explanation of the items in your purse, in particular the encrypted phone, its purpose, and who you really are, was an unexpected windfall. I leave for home very soon. You will be coming with me. And what I shall obtain for you will more than make up for my losses."

Maur reentered the room carrying a medium-sized aluminum case. He placed the case on a side counter next to a sink, released twin clasps, and opened the lid. He removed heavy black welder's gloves and pulled each on tight. He reached into the case again and produced a propane torch and striker. He turned the valve on the torch and sparked the striker. A translucent blue flame hissed. He adjusted the valve to concentrate the flame and set the torch aside. His gloved hand went back into the case and drew out a two-foot-long black cloth sleeve. He undid a drawstring and pulled out a branding iron. The branding iron tip formed the letter M.

Maur carried the torch and the branding iron to Molka's side. He held both above her head and put the flame to the branding iron tip.

Molka watched the tip smoke with an unthinkable smell. The smoke dissipated, and the tip began to glow dark orange.

Molka looked to Sago. He turned away and headed toward the door. "I never stay for this part. I am brave enough to admit I am a coward."

CHAPTER TWENTY-THREE

"**D**on't start, Warren," Nadia said.

"Why not?" Warren said. "We're only a few minutes away. And I have a great idea. Pest Control turned in their equipment last night. I have it in the trunk. Coveralls, hats, sprayers. We can go over there and do an overt entry. I'll take the outside, you take the inside. Our old trick. Maybe even see if we can get him to take some selfies with us that we can show at the Christmas party. It will be fun."

"We don't have a truck though."

"You think that troll is going to look outside for a truck? Come on, let's hurry up and go do it."

Nadia took off her sunglasses, opened her eyes, and squinted at Warren in the lounge chair next to her. "What's wrong with you?"

"We left Lawn Service to close it out."

"And? He's leaving. He's practically gone. Lawn Service can handle another two...," she grabbed Warren's wrist and viewed his watch, "another one hour and forty-one minutes."

"We should do a final check anyway. Just to be safe."

Nadia held up her phone. "Do you know what the current temperature is? It's 77°F. Do you know what the current temperature is at Reagan National? It's 34°F. Want to know what the temperature is going to be there when we land tomorrow? 31°F."

"What's your point?"

"My point is, this is a warm beach. This is a hot new bikini. This is a cold drink. And this is the first unscheduled day off we've taken in over a year."

"That's what I'm really worried about," Warren said. "The unscheduled part. I think we should at least double check the airport."

"It's done. I took care of it while you were at the gym this morning."

"You did? Please brief me."

Nadia shifted her made-for-bikini body onto its side toward Warren. "Sago had all his baggage except for one personal set loaded on his aircraft last night. His pilots checked out of their hotel at 10AM and are at the airport, probably doing their preflight as we speak. Departure forecast: excellent. The aircraft's been washed, fueled, and its galley fully stocked right down to a case of pooch pads for his mutts to poop on."

"That's outstanding work, partner."

"Always. But no more work today. Enjoy yourself a little. Order a beer or something."

"What about the message our friend left a little while ago? Shouldn't we call back and find out what he wants?"

"I know what he wants," Nadia said. "He wants to ask us if we can help them spring their girl. Again, taken care of."

"I know. But shouldn't we still—"

"Stop feeling guilty. Things broke our way for once. Probably never happen again. So, relax. Let me relax. Op's over."

Warren took in the ocean view. "Guess you're right."

"Damn right, I'm right."

Warren stood. "I'm going to check in with Lawn Service anyway."

Nadia sighed. "Whatever."

"And I'm going to call our friend back and ask what he wants."

"Go right ahead." Nadia jammed her sunglasses back on. "And while you do I'm going to lay here and get a base tan today, even if I have to piss off every warlord in Central Asia to do it."

"You already did that once."

"Don't start, Warren."

 CHAPTER TWENTY-FOUR

"**I** very badly want to burn out one of your eyes," Maur said. "That would please me greatly." He swung the branding iron above Molka's face like a pendulum, and her eyes tracked the searing bright orange M at the tip. "How would the pretty whore feel about wearing an eye patch for the rest of her life to cover her deformity?"

"Proud," Molka said. "I grew up idolizing a man who wore an eyepatch."

Maur laughed. "False bravado. The last line of defense against absolute terror."

Defense already breached.

"I will admit you are different," Maur said. "They all beg me pathetically at this point not to burn them. You cannot imagine the offers I have received. And promises to do the vilest things I suggested. They begged to do them. What promise will you make me?"

"I'll tell you later. But you might not like it."

Maur bent and whispered in Molka's ear. "No, whore. You will tell me now. And you will beg me now. And I will like it. You will beg to live. And you will beg to die. Death better than living. Living worse than death. But I will leave you with something much more unbearable: eternal fear."

Maur straightened and lowered the M inches above Molka's left eye.

Molka closed both eyes against the singeing heat and attacked the restraints, but it was pointless.

Burning's better than drowning, right? Maybe not.

Waiting to burn.

Hating to burn.

Nothing burned.

The heat reduced.

Molka opened her eyes.

Maur held the tip pointed up. "Mr. Sago has forbidden me to mar your face in any way. He said you are not like the others I have entertained. He said I must not devalue his commodity. So, sadly, I will not be able to burn out your eye."

Molka allowed relief to comfort her.

Maur stepped over to the side sink and placed the branding iron in it. He pulled off his gloves, took a foot-long black tactical knife from his aluminum case, and went back to Molka. "But, Mr. Sago has also said every great artist should sign his work." He centered the tip over her left eye. Molka reconsidered begging, but there was no time. Maur plunged the knife. Molka flinched. The knife stuck in the table alongside her head. Maur smiled and undid the top three buttons on Molka's dress, exposing her bra. He unstuck the knife and cut the bra in half between her breasts, severed both shoulder straps, yanked the bra from her body, and dropped it on the floor.

Molka braced herself for rape. Again.

Maur went back to the sink and returned wearing the gloves and holding the branding iron.

He held the tip over Molka's face.

Molka braced herself for terror. Again.

"When your new owner is done with you," Maur said, "if he allows you to live, you will likely be sold into the most wretched whorehouses of the world. There, you can tell all those who will still have you that, the M wound you carry stands for Molka. But you and I will always know that it stands for Maur. I will place my mark where you will see it and feel it every day, until you die. And you will see me and feel me every day, until you die."

Maur lowered the scorching M six inches above Molka's left nipple and paused.

Molka fought screaming. She lost.

Maur laughed. Savored. Loving that part. Her screaming.

Molka stopped screaming and listened.

A buzzing.

Are they coming?

A growling.

They are coming.

A rumbling.

They're here!

The deep throated arrival roar of twenty angry Harleys.

Maur cocked an ear to the rising clamor.

Sago tripped into the room. "Stop that and come immediately!" He stumbled back out.

Maur's dark eyes reviled into Molka. She waited for him to disobey his master's order. She knew he wanted to—maybe more than anything he ever wanted. But he couldn't. The insecurity of his strength made him firmly weak. He dropped the branding iron into the sink and ran after Sago.

Molka waited.

Struggled.

Panicked.

Recovered.

Remembered.

She yelled:

"LOTO!"

"LOTO!"

"LOTO!"

Loto's voice from within the mansion, "Molka? Molka, where are you?"

She yelled again:

"KILL HIM!"

"KILL HIM!"

"KILL HIM!"

CHAPTER TWENTY-FIVE

Sago cowered in the entry hall, hugging his trembling children. Through the large front windows all three watched the two-wheeled carnage.

Six motorcycle riders spun doughnuts on the front lawn tearing black scars in the emerald perfection. Another rider plowed through the flower beds throwing up a dirt and flora rooster tail. Still another rider dismounted and urinated into the fountain with a demonic laugh. A dozen other riders lapped the circular driveway in a deafening, maniacal race.

Maur ran to Sago's side. "Should I call the police, sir?"

"I would assume the neighbors have already done so."

"Yes, sir."

Sago pointed to the mayhem. "And spewed from the corrupted grave he did leer; ride Vindicator ride, go forth in noble folly, and smite the wicked righteous. The Retribution of Franklin O'Donnell. Last act. Final scene."

"Sir?" Maur said.

"Franklin did business with these gangs for years. Methamphetamine. Two days ago, he boasted of powerful new friends. Friends not to be betrayed. A veiled warning to me, of course. Now these new friends—these barbarians, these

Vindicators—blame me for his disappearance. Is that not obvious?"

"Yes, sir."

"Your assessment of this behavior?"

"A diversion, sir." Maur said. "The main attack will come from another direction."

"Then let us not wait for the main attack. We will leave for the airport immediately. Drive around them if we can. Drive over them if we must."

"Yes, sir. What about the whore, sir?"

"Leave her to them. A fitting fate." Glass shattered in the mansion rear. "They are coming inside! Give me the car keys. Meet us in the car. Bring only your pistol. Get it now!"

"Yes, sir." Maur handed Sago the keys and bolted and rumbled up the stairs.

Sago opened the door and hesitated before the havoc. Screaming came from within the house; Molka's voice. A deep male voice called out to her.

Sago yelled up the staircase, "Maur, hurry!"

Maur thundered back down the stairs, pistol held high.

At the entry hall's far end, Sago spotted a massive brown blur dashing toward them.

Maur spotted it too. Too late.

Loto roared into Maur. Six hundred combined pounds collided and hit the floor with the force of a bridge collapse.

Maur fumbled his pistol, and it skidded across the marble.

Sago stepped back, watched the pistol slide next to the wall, making no move to retrieve it.

Loto and Maur recovered and got to their feet simultaneously, their free-style wrestling instincts triggered.

Loto struck first. He tackled Maur's legs, lifted him, pancaked him onto his back, and went for a quick pin.

Maur rolled onto his stomach, pushed up to his hands and knees, stood with Loto clinging to his back, bulldozed Loto into the stairs, breaking his hold, and then grabbed his own lower back in pain.

Loto pushed off the stairs, got to his feet, and coiled to jump on Maur's injured back.

Maur spun around, uninjured, crouched, and dove for Loto's legs.

Loto bent at the waist, pressed down on Maur's charging shoulders, and side stepped clear, like a nose tackle shedding a center's cut block. Maur face-planted into the bottom step and stayed down, disorientated.

Loto grabbed Maur around the waist from behind with both arms. "I was ready for your lame-ass deke this time; you hack. Now check this out." Loto lifted Maur up and off the floor, crouched, fired his thighs, arched his back, and tossed Maur up and over his head.

Maur's skull THRACKED on the marble. His body followed, crumpling onto itself followed by Loto crumpling onto him, completing a devastating belly-to-back suplex. Maur lay motionless.

Loto stood and looked at a mortified Sago. "Won my second state title with that move. Where's Molka?"

Sago pointed a trembling finger. "She is in the laundry room."

"Your man has a hard head," Loto said. "It's not even cut from that drop. But he's probably concussed. He'll need a nice long quiet rest for that. I'll help him on his way."

Loto sat Maur up, got behind him, looped his right arm around Maur's neck—catching Maur's throat in the crook of his arm—and reached across and grabbed his own left bicep.

Rear chokehold locked in.

Maur's face blossomed red. His eyes opened and boiled, his forehead veins near bursting. Mouth opened to take in air the choked off neck would not allow.

Loto held his grip.

Maur's eyes closed.

Loto tightened his grip.

Maur's body relaxed.

Loto maximized his grip.

Maur's body slumped, limp.

Loto laid Maur's body face down.

Sago collected his children and ran out the door.

CHAPTER TWENTY-SIX

"**D**id you kill him?" Molka said.

"I put him down," Loto said.

"Is he dead?"

"He won't hurt you anymore."

Loto undid the straps and Molka slid off the table. "Where's Sago?"

"He locked himself in his car. The Brothers have him blocked in."

Loto trailed Molka's run from the laundry room, through the pantry, through the kitchen, through the dining room, across the entry hall, past Maur's motionless body, and out the front door. The members, most still on their bikes, surrounded Sago's Mercedes.

Molka bounded down the steps and looked inside the car. Sago cringed in the backseat with his dogs.

"Does he have the car keys or a phone?" Molka said.

"He has the keys," Ramrod said. "If he has a phone, he hasn't used it."

"That means he probably doesn't. Alright. Get the keys away from him. Break the window if you have to."

"What about his dogs?" Ramrod said.

"Leave them with him," Molka said. "It will help keep him calm. I need to run back inside and get my bag." She bounded back up the steps.

"Hey Molka?" Loto said.

Molka stopped and turned. "What's wrong?"

Loto smiled. "You did it. You got him. Your plan worked."

Molka smiled back and ran through the front door, past Maur's body, and up the stairs into the study. She scanned the furniture and tables. No bag. She searched the large desk. Nothing. She checked the bookcases. Not there. Then she found it. Outside the French Doors on the balcony table, beside an ash tray with one of Sago's half-smoked brown cigarettes, sat her bag, both her weapons, and both her phones. She tossed everything in the bag, ran back through the study, down the stairs, into the entry hall, and STOPPED.

Maur's body was missing.

Molka's eyes caught movement outside the open front door: Sago's Mercedes leaving. She ran onto the porch. All the members lay face-down in the driveway, ankles crossed, bikes on their sides next to them. The Mercedes rolled, not in a rush, toward the gate.

Molka pulled her Beretta, assumed a combat stance, and aimed at the right rear tire.

"No, Miss Molka!" Ramrod said. "They took Baby!" Ramrod and the members scrambled to their feet. "The big man surprised us. He's got a gun on Baby. Fat man's driving."

Molka leapt off the porch and ran to her car. Two tires were knifed flat. "No!"

"He made me do that," Cuda said.

All watched the Mercedes reach the front gate. The brake lights lit up, and the car rocked to a halt.

The back-passenger door opened.

Loto climbed out.

The door slammed shut.

The back-passenger window lowered.

Loto turned to face the car.

Unheard words were exchanged.

A pistoled hand thrust from the window.

Loto stepped back and stumbled sideways.

Two rapid shots.
Loto fell.
The car shrieked out of the gate.
Molka screamed, "NO! YOU BASTARD! NO!"

CHAPTER TWENTY-SEVEN

Molka sprinted to Loto. Ramrod and the members followed.
Loto sprawled on his back—conscious but grimacing. Molka
knelt and located the wounds. One grazed his upper left thigh.
Not too bad. The other penetrated his huge abdomen. He wasn't
bleeding much. Was that a good thing? She wasn't sure. But a
medic had once told her to never get shot in the belly. It usually
ended badly.

Distant police sirens approached.

"Someone finally woke up the cops," Ramrod said. "Time to
go."

"They'll call paramedics," Molka said. "I'll stay with him."

"It'll be quicker if we take him," Radical said. "St. Joes
Hospital is right over the bridge."

Ramrod faced the gathered members. "Get the van up here!
And bring me my bike! The rest of you, boogie!"

The members scattered to obey.

"Sorry, Molka," Loto said. "I couldn't kill him. You know
me; I try to love everyone. I'm just a humble man of peace."

Molka smiled. "Don't think of it. Be still."

The van smoked tires in reverse and locked up the brakes next to Loto. Bronco and Detroit jumped out and opened the back doors.

"What about them?" Bronco pointed at the two fake lawn service men zip cuffed on the floor.

"Cut 'em loose," Ramrod said.

Detroit cut them loose.

"Can I have my phone back?" the driver said.

Ramrod nodded, and Bronco tossed it to him. The fake lawn service men jogged back toward their truck.

Bronco, Detroit, and Ramrod lifted Loto and laid him in the van.

"Molka?" Loto said.

"Yes, Loto."

"I know I owe you, but maybe do me another favor?"

"Of course."

"If you get the chance someday, kill that Maur guy for me."

Molka reached into the van and took Loto's hand. "If I get the chance, someday will be today."

CHAPTER TWENTY-EIGHT

The Vindicators MC fled White Sands Mansion. Milwaukee-made power poured out the front gate. Cave Monster rode Ramrod's Sportster to where Ramrod and Molka stood, put it on the kickstand, and ran back to get his own ride.

"I'm taking your bike," Molka said.

"The hell you are," Ramrod said.

"I need it. I'm going after them."

"I need it. I'm going after them."

"To do what?"

"Whatever I have to!" Ramrod said. "I'll run the sons of bitches off the road! Into a ditch, into a power pole, into the god damned Atlantic if I have to!"

"You don't know where they're going. I do."

"You have no way to get there. I do."

"This is my family's feud. Not your business."

Ramrod pointed at Loto's blood on the driveway. "That makes it my business."

"I'm taking your bike. I'm sorry." Molka stepped back and pulled the Beretta from her bag.

Ramrod frowned. "Really?"

"No." Molka put the gun back in her bag. "Not really."

Ramrod mounted and started his bike. He looked at Molka. The coming sirens were much closer. "Well, prospect, get on." She slung her bag over her shoulder and did. "Which way?"

The thirty-five-minute ride up I-95 remained lawless, even as they traveled at speeds approaching its namesake. But when they exited onto the road leading to the airport, the first thing they passed was a carwash. And the only thing being washed was a sheriff's department motorcycle, by a deputy and fellow Harley rider. He admired Ramrod's Sportster and nodded. Ramrod didn't return the respect. They rode on.

Molka noted a sign: **South Florida Regional Executive Airport - 8 Miles.** She checked her watch: 1:26 PM. Thirty-four minutes till Sago was wheels up and gone forever.

They passed another deputy sheriff, a cruiser posted in a fast food parking lot. Not eating. Watching. He spotted what he watched for, pulled out, slid in behind them, and lit the lightbar.

Ramrod juiced the throttle. The deputy's cruiser in the side mirror got small fast. Ramrod laughed and raised a defiant fist. He checked the mirror again, lowered his fist, cursed, slowed, banked into another fast food parking lot, and shut it down.

"Why are we stopping?" Molka said.

"Miss Molka, I've run from the law enough times to know you usually don't get away without a fight."

"I'm not afraid to fight. Keep going!"

Ramrod shook his head. "Call me old school, but I won't put a civilian female at risk. On the other hand, no sense in us both going to jail either. When he takes me off the bike, I'm going to get his attention, and you haul ass."

"Alright."

The deputy rolled in behind them, stopped, and talked on his radio.

"Listen up," Ramrod said. "This machine's a lot heavier than the CBR600 you rode. Watch your turns. And go easy on the takeoff."

"Yes, sir. Sorry about all the trouble I've caused you guys."

"Just get us some payback for Baby. He's a great kid. Ok, here he comes. Good luck."

Molka hugged him from behind. "Thanks for everything, Ramrod."

The serious young deputy approached from their left rear, hand on sidearm. When he got alongside Ramrod, his face broke into amusement. "I don't believe it. Ramrod Yates? Is that really you? It is. This is a real blast from the past. Nice to see you're still kicking. How many years has it been since we ran you out of this county?"

Ramrod snorted. "That'll be the day when a kid your age runs me outta anywhere. Don't you have a paper route to go finish, sonny?"

"You're behind the times, Yates. We kids don't read newspapers. We get all our info real time. And it just came across my computer that a bunch of big bad bikers were tearing up someone's yard down in Cinnamon Cove. Shots fired too. Know anything about that?"

Ramrod looked at the deputy's badge and smirked. "Nope. Me and my old lady were just out for a leisurely afternoon ride."

"She's your old lady?" The deputy smiled. "She looks more like your old lady's daughter's daughter."

"You're funny, deputy. About as funny as road rash on my ball sack. Now can we get on with this?"

"Here's what's going to happen, Yates. When I tell you, I want you to stand up slowly. And then you're going to walk over and put your hands on the hood of my car. And then you're going into cuffs."

"For what?"

"For my safety while I do an investigation. You're a convicted felon." The deputy turned to Molka. "Miss, when he gets off the motorcycle, I don't want you to move. You just sit there and place your hands on the handlebars until I say otherwise. Do you understand?"

Molka smiled. "Yes, deputy."

"Stand up, Yates."

Ramrod dismounted, walked to the deputy's car, and put his hands on the hood with legs spread, looking like he had done it a few times before. The deputy patted him down, cuffed him, leaned him against the front grill, and talked into the speaker mic clipped to his shirt.

Ramrod straitened, stepped back, and started to jog toward the fast food building.

"Stop!" the deputy yelled and ran after him. "Stop, Yates! Don't make me shoot you!" He drew his weapon.

Ramrod stopped before he reached the door. Then he turned around, sank to his knees, and smiled at Molka.

Molka hit the starter, squeezed the clutch, dropped it into gear, released the clutch, and twisted the throttle. The Sportster leapt forward with so much unexpected torque she almost lost her grip. She wobbled, recovered, and rode for the exit. The deputy yelled at her, but the engine roar swallowed his words. She flashed by him and got back on the airport road.

Molka wished for eye protection. Florida was a no helmet law state—good for visibility, but bad for eyes and face in the stinging sandy air.

Squint. Tough it out. Almost there.

Two blocks down, the motorcycle deputy from the carwash passed her coming the other way. In the mirror Molka, watched him slow, U-turn, put on a blue light, and accelerate after her.

Molka cut to the right down a residential side street.

The deputy followed.

She cut to the left down another street.

The deputy followed.

She cut right and left down two more streets.

The deputy followed and followed.

He was good and gaining.

She wasn't skilled enough a rider to elude him. She needed another option.

Stop and neutralize?

Maybe. But knocking out casino security personnel with orders not to hurt her was one thing. Knocking out a sworn officer of the law was quite another. He was authorized to fight back—with deadly force, no less. No, the situation called for a more creative solution: what her American Captain referred to as, "The employment of a dynamic but nuanced combination of advanced strategic, operational, and tactical planning.

Translation: if you can't dazzle them with brilliance, baffle them with bullshit."

Molka eased into an alley beside a convenience store and stopped. The deputy pulled in and parked fifteen feet behind her. She left the bike running, put it on the kickstand, reverse leap frogged off, and spun to face the still seated deputy. She smiled. He didn't. She skipped over to his bike, located the ignition key, switched it off, removed it, tossed it in her bag, and said, "Sorry, handsome. I know this is going to be very embarrassing for you tonight at the sheriff's bar."

"Where?" the deputy said.

She skipped back, forward leap frogged onto the bike, and peeked over her shoulder. "But I just don't have time for anything more clever."

"What?" The deputy placed his hand on his weapon.

She smiled again. "You wouldn't shoot a fellow Harley rider, would you?"

"Who?"

Molka popped a little wheelie on takeoff and tore around the building. She almost rear ended a car waiting to exit the parking lot. She weaved around it and bumped over a curb into moving traffic.

A car swerved to miss her.

Then another.

Then another.

Horns shouted.

Vulgarities blasted.

Middle fingers raised.

Molka went full throttle and left them all behind.

About six miles to the airport.

She glanced at her watch again.

Twenty-two minutes left.

# CHAPTER TWENTY-NINE

It wasn't a great plan, or even a good one. But it was the best one Molka could think of in the five-minute ride to the airport.

It went like this:

Phase One: Get aboard Sago's aircraft.

Phase Two: Kill Maur.

Phase Three: Deliver Sago, by any means necessary, to the contractor team.

Molka parked and shut off the bike. The South Florida Regional Executive Airport didn't live up to its big name. She reconnoitered a small terminal, some hangers, a few maintenance buildings, and two long runways.

She took out her encrypted phone and messaged the contractor team:

Current status?

Still waiting at casino hotel.

Stand-by for delivery.

Molka dismounted and ran through the terminal's automatic doors into a quiet waiting area. She crossed to large windows in back that looked out on the runways. Sago's private jet was parked on the far side, impossible to miss; it was the biggest aircraft in sight, gleaming white with a black stripe running its length. A black tail featured the initials GS in gold script. Three things next to it interested her. Boarding stairs attached to the front exit door. Why were they still there? Maintenance stairs against the port engine. A possible problem? And a twice occupied SUV with the word SECURITY in white letters above the front windshield. A definite problem.

She applied the new intel to her plan. Security personnel must be neutralized, obviously. A firefight was out of the question. So was a fistfight. Maur might see it.

She checked her watch. Sixteen minutes left.

But no time to plan and execute another diversion either. Sixteen minutes left.

Molka reached behind her head and tugged at the base of her ponytail.

Think.

Sixteen minutes left.

There must be a way to…

Sixteen minutes left.

I can't see how…

Sixteen minutes left.

He's going to escape!

Calm slipped toward panic slipped toward hysterics.

Hysterics. What did her mother say about hysterical people? The goal of a hysterical person is to draw attention to themselves, and to their dilemma, from people who don't know them and are more likely to give a sympathetic response. This behavior can manipulate total strangers into serving the hysterical person's needs. Sounded logical. Worth a try.

Molka located the airport office, ran to it, and ripped open the door. A middle-aged woman worked at a desk.

"May I help you?" the woman said.

Molka yelled. "WHO'S IN CHARGE HERE?"

"Mr. Gomez is the airport manager."

"WHERE IS HE?"

"He's in a meeting."

"CALL HIM NOW! IT'S AN EMERGENCY! CALL SECURITY TOO!"

"He's meeting with the security chief."

"CALL THEM NOW!"

An inner office door behind the woman opened. A heavyset Hispanic man in a brown suit stepped out. A tall, lean older white man wearing a tan police-style uniform and an armed duty belt followed him.

The Hispanic man said, "What's the problem, miss?"

"WHO ARE YOU?"

"I'm Joe Gomez, the airport manager. Please calm down, miss."

"YOU MUST NOT LET THAT AIRCRAFT LEAVE!"

"Please calm down, miss. What aircraft are you talking about?"

"GASZI SAGO'S PRIVATE JET. DO NOT LET IT TAKEOFF!"

"Please stop yelling, miss. We want to help you. What do you think is wrong with Mr. Sago's aircraft?"

"Nothing. But a man on the aircraft, Sago's man, assaulted me and shot my friend today. DO NOT LET THEM TAKE OFF! GIVE THE ORDER NOW! THEY LEAVE IN SIXTEEN," Molka checked her watch, "IN FIFTEEN MINUTES!"

"You must please stop yelling and calm down, miss. We can't help you if you don't calm down. Will you calm down? Will you let us help you?"

Hysterics worked. Thanks, mom.

"Yes," Molka said, "I'll let you help me."

"Good. This is Ed Reynolds, our security chief."

Reynolds said, "You claim someone on Mr. Sago's aircraft assaulted you and a friend?"

"Assaulted me and shot my friend. That's why you can't allow it to takeoff in fifteen minutes."

Gomez said, "Mr. Sago's aircraft will not be departing in fifteen minutes."

"Why not?" Molka said.

"The FAA has asked for a ramp check."

"What's a ramp check?"

"It's a routine compliance inspection."

"What does that mean?"

"It means the aircraft won't be leaving for several more hours. The inspectors aren't even here yet. They've been delayed.

So, you see, there's nothing to be worried about. Just stay calm, please."

Reynolds said, "Do you know the name of the man you say assaulted your friend and you?"

"Shot my friend. Assaulted me. Yes, it's Maur."

"They've already cleared customs," Gomez said. "Let's check the manifest and see if he's listed." Molka and Reynolds followed Gomez back into his office. He sat at the desk and accessed his computer. "I have Mr. Sago, a Captain, a First Officer, and a Doctor Maur."

"Doctor Maur?" Molka said.

"Yes," Gomez said. "Doctor Maur. Mr. Sago and his wife's personal physician."

Molka loosed a sarcastic laugh. "Let me tell you about my experience with *Doctor Maur* today. His examination table is a waterboard. And his preferred treatment for me is a branding iron. Then he made a house call in a driveway and prescribed my friend two gunshots to the lower body."

"Those are very serious charges," Reynolds said. "Can you positively identify this man?"

"Yes, yes. Bring him to me, and I will positively identify him for you. But be careful. He's armed and insane."

"We have no authority to board Mr. Sago's aircraft," Gomez said.

"If this is a criminal matter," Reynolds said, "maybe you would want to speak with the sheriff's department?"

No, she wouldn't want to speak with the sheriff's department. But at least two of them would want to speak with her. After she was in custody.

"Not yet," Molka said. "You're right; these are very serious charges. Could you ask Mr. Sago to send his doctor to this office? If I identify him as the same man who assaulted me and shot my friend, you could hold him for local law enforcement."

"What do you think, Joe?" Reynolds said.

"Mr. Sago is a valued customer," Gomez said. "I wouldn't want to inconvenience him unnecessarily. Perhaps we could go ask Mr. Sago if he would be willing to produce his passenger. If Mr. Sago agrees, and if she identifies him as the man who committed these alleged crimes, then like she said, your men can detain him for the sheriff. Let them sort it out."

"Ok, sounds good," Reynolds said. He took out and talked into his radio, "Bobby, Nick, come to the terminal. Code silver."

His radio talked back, "Copy."

"What's a code silver?" Molka said.

"It means come in a hurry. My men will escort us. You said this individual is dangerous."

Reynolds men arrived: the same duo parked in the SUV guarding Sago's jet, both younger and wearing the same tan uniform. They picked up Molka, Reynolds, and Gomez at the terminal's rear entrance and drove them across the tarmac.

On the way Molka modified her plan:

Phase One: Get them to detain Maur.

Phase Two: Deliver Sago to the contractor team.

Phase Three: Come back and kill Maur.

The SUV parked, and everyone exited. Gomez told all to wait and went up the stairs and into the aircraft. Molka moved behind the SUV putting the engine block between herself and the jet.

"I would advise you men to take cover," Molka said. "This maniac is capable of anything. He might come out firing."

Reynolds stood with one hand behind his back. "I think we'll be fine, miss. Just stay calm."

Two minutes later Gomez descended the stairs followed by Sago and Maur. The pair had changed into traveling clothes. Sago now wore a blue blazer over an open-collar mauve shirt. Maur wore a tight white polo that accentuated his menacing muscles.

Molka pointed. "That's the man. The big ugly one. I mean the taller big ugly one. Positive identification."

Gomez and Sago stepped off the stairs and moved aside, leaving Maur on the last step. The two younger security men drew their weapons and pointed them at Maur.

Reynolds said, "Freeze. Put your hands up."

Maur froze and put his hands up.

Molka came from behind the SUV. She strode up to Maur and stopped too close. Her blue eyes sliced up into his. His dark eyes sliced down into hers.

"You asked me what I would promise you," Molka said. "So, here it is: Whatever cage they put you in now, little doggie. I'll come back and take you out later. Sooner than later. And then you'll beg me. I promise."

Maur smiled. "Eternal fear."

"Code silver," Reynolds said.

The two security men pivoted and aimed their weapons at Molka.

Instincts plunged Molka's right hand toward her bag.

Her hand never made it.

Reynolds stepped behind her and deployed a Taser into her back.

Molka screeched and arched in pain. Her eyes closed over an anguished face. Her knees caved.

The two security men holstered their weapons and caught her as she fell.

Reynolds continued to click electric agony into her body.

One count.

Two count.

Three count.

It ended.

They laid a dazed Molka on her stomach.

Reynolds knelt and removed the Taser darts from Molka's back.

"Dr. Maur" came forward with a syringe and jabbed Molka's bare upper right arm. Her daze slipped into abrupt paralysis and extreme fatigue. Unconsciousness loomed.

Before reality became dark and soundless, she heard them talking about her.

Sago said, "I apologize, gentlemen, for asking you to go along with my subterfuge, and to use such a drastic method. But if you will look in her bag you will see the disturbing items I spoke of."

Maur reached into Molka's bag and removed the Beretta and Glock.

Sago went on, "She is quite unstable and prone to violent outbursts. I think this was best for all our safety."

"I agree," Reynolds said.

"She showed up hysterical," Gomez said. "Told us Doctor Maur assaulted her and shot her friend. Exactly as you said she would."

"My wife is a sick woman. Dangerously sick, I am afraid. I thank you for bringing her to me. Now, if I could impose further and ask the assistance of your men in carrying her aboard, Doctor Maur will make her comfortable."

"It's such a shame," Gomez said. "I hope your wife gets the help she deserves when you get her back home."

Sago suppressed a smile. "Yes. When I get her back home, I will make sure she gets exactly what she deserves."

CHAPTER THIRTY

It was the most comfortable chair she had ever sat in, with oversized, butter-soft white leather cushions. A matching chair faced her. To her right were two identical chairs across a gold-carpeted aisle which ended at a cherrywood door with a gold handle. The first-class sleeper area in Sago's private aircraft smelled of leather, furniture polish, and Sago's scented brown cigarettes.

Molka woke strapped tight to the chair and wearing a straitjacket. Her ankles shackled together and a ball gag filling her mouth completed the restraint. It was a little much. But after all, she was considered a dangerously sick woman. Her hair scrunchy, tac-boots, and socks were missing, but her pilot's watch and Loto's necklace were not. She never got a chance to ask Maur why he chose to remove and leave these things. She looked out the window to her left. The boarding steps were still attached, but the security SUV was gone. There was no need for it; the threat had been contained. Sago was safe.

A door at the compartment rear opened, and Sago approached up the aisle. He sat in the chair across from Molka and smiled. "Awake already, I see. You have a stronger constitution than the others who have experienced Maur's needle.

I am going to remove the gag. If you begin to scream, I will have Maur come gag you with something much more unpleasant. Is that understood?"

Molka nodded, and he unbuckled the leather strap and set the gag on the cushion next to her.

Sago brushed the bangs from Molka's eyes. "I wonder, will the next one they send to kill me be so beautiful? No, it is not possible."

"I didn't come to kill you," Molka said.

"Not as such. But certainly, that would have been the end result had you succeeded."

"Why did you have my friend shot?"

"To assure you would come after me and be sitting here at this moment."

Molka squirmed in the straitjacket. "You really want me that bad?"

"Your personal worth to me has become inconsequential." Sago took out and lit a cigarette from a gold case in his jacket pocket. "You are now simply an object which I possess."

"Don't you mean an untraditional commodity?"

"Yes. An untraditional commodity I will trade for something of greater value to me. What is important from this point on is the interest of your bidders. And I must say that interest is substantial."

"Because you've told these bidders all about me."

"I have told them nothing about you yet. I only made them aware I have something of exceptional quality. Since my reputation for quality is beyond reproach, this alone has started a bidder's war. A war on which I will further capitalize when I release the true nature of your value."

"And capitalizing on war seems to be your true nature."

Sago smiled. "Well put, beautiful one. However, not accurate. My business is purely business. I consider myself completely apolitical."

"Yet you assisted the Traitors."

Sago's smile left. "No. They acted in their own self interests. As we all do. I merely obtained their information, traded it to interested parties, and took a profit."

"That information you profited from had names. And husbands and wives and children and mothers and fathers and brothers and little sisters and hopes and dreams."

"They were spies, committing illegal acts in foreign countries."

"They were patriots."

Sago waved an indifferent hand. "Patriots, traitors, traitors, patriots—these are emotional terms of conscience. Conscience has no place in the successful trader."

"Even a death trader?"

Sago scowled into a smile. "Do you recall the story I told you from my boyhood in which my grandfather's watch was taken from me and destroyed by the boys from a street gang?"

"Yes, and please don't tell me you're going to lay this all on being bullied as a kid. Because that's a really overused excuse."

"I have never made excuses for my actions. But getting back to my story, after they took the beloved watch, I was at my wits end. I decided I must either drown myself in the Danube or go to the leader of the gang and make a deal. I chose the latter and offered him my services. Not for use as a thug—of which I was ill suited—rather the use of my intellect. After having me beaten several times, he listened to my proposal."

Sago inhaled his cigarette, nose exhaled smoke, and went on, "I showed this gang how to move away from petty street crimes, and onto more elaborate and lucrative burglaries. These same boys who tormented me, came to admire my talents. Later, I used them to depose our leader and install me as their new master."

"To show them my gratitude, I planned a major theft from a prestigious auction house. This auction house was storing several million dollars' worth of artworks from an upcoming estate sale. I told them I would sell the treasures to a wealthy Russian oligarch and make us all rich. During the commission of the robbery—of which I was not present—they brutally murdered an off-duty policeman serving as a night watchman. I may have failed to inform them about the presence of the policeman. Nevertheless, they carried off the rest of my plan to perfection."

Sago flicked ash into a gold armrest ashtray. "After I had the trove of near priceless objects hidden away, I went to the police and offered to give them the identity of the robbers and murderers in exchange for unconditional immunity for myself. They agreed. Next, I went to the owners of the auction house and offered to return the artworks in exchange for no questions asked, a cash reward, full funding of my university education, and a new Jaguar convertible, silver. They agreed. The boys received life sentences. This was my first major deal. I was seventeen years old."

"Now, you tell me, was I wrong to get my revenge and rid the world of such violent vermin, while at the same time securing a better future for myself?"

"No," Molka said. "Not necessarily. But…a snitch is still a snitch. And snitches are all hated to some extent, even if what they did was morally right."

"You begin to understand, beautiful one. Moral decisions are not always perfectly moral. They can sometimes be messy, dirty, ugly things. But we all must make them, and we all must live with them. Once you have accepted this, there comes some measure of inner peace."

Molka frowned. "Do you ever think about what you could have been?"

"Frequently." Sago stubbed out his cigarette and smiled. "How do you like my aircraft?"

"Impressive. Beautiful. What a way to go."

Sago laughed. "Even now, she still delights." He leaned forward and replaced the gag. "Once we are airborne, I will give you a proper tour."

Sago left through the forward cherrywood door. Molka looked out the window again. Two men waited next to the boarding stairs, each wearing a white pilot shirt and a black tie. One's shoulder boards displayed four gold stripes, the other's shoulder boards three gold stripes: the aircraft's captain and first officer.

A white van with red FAA logos on the doors arrived and parked across from the stairs. A female driver and male passenger stepped out. Both put on blue windbreakers with the letters "FAA" emblazed in gold on the back. The delayed inspectors had arrived. The captain and first officer greeted them with handshakes. Sago waddled down the stairs and spoke to the inspectors. The male inspector checked his watch and spoke to

Sago. Sago turned and re-waddled up into the aircraft. The female inspector spoke to the pilots and pointed at the terminal. The pilots nodded and followed the inspectors toward the building.

The inspectors were Nadia and Warren.

Molka smiled behind the gag. Was there no end to their amazing resources? And their dedication was admirable. Loyal corporate minions to the end, personally assuring that everything was in order and Sago would leave US soil alive and coherent.

Congratulations. You did your jobs well. Soon you will be rid of Mr. Gaszi Sago forever.

And of me too.

CHAPTER THIRTY-ONE

Molka back-talked to Maur. "You must think I'm a real dangerous woman."

Thirty minutes into the flight—at Maur's gunpoint—an unshackled, ungagged, and un-straitjacketed Molka entered Sago's flying office: a large compartment decorated with more white leather, cherrywood, gold accents, and an oversized desk.

Maur directed Molka to a chair across from the desk. She sat and watched him position himself on a side couch with the pistol on his lap, staring and mute.

The only sounds were the muffled roar of jet engines and the sharp ticking of an antique clock on the desk.

Tick.

Tick.

Tick.

"Where's your master?" Molka said.

Maur stared at her, mute.

Tick.

Tick.

Tick.

"He and his *children* hiding from you? Can't blame them."

Maur stared at her, mute.

Tick.

Tick.

Tick.

"What did you inject me with?"

Maur stared at her, mute.

Tick.

Tick.

Tick.

"What's wrong, past your feeding time?"

Maur stared at her, mute.

Tick.

Tick.

Tick.

"Why don't you put that weapon away? You've already shot one good man today."

Maur stared at her, mute.

Tick.

Tick.

Tick.

Sago and his dogs entered from a rear door. His dogs left him and wagged straight to Molka. She petted them.

Sago sat behind his desk and smiled at Molka. "You look much more comfortable and relaxed now, beautiful one."

"Not quite," Molka said and nodded at Maur. "You should tell him to stow his weapon. Bullets and pressurized cabins don't mix. And it's not like I'm going to break for the door and make a run for it at 35,000 feet."

"Even if you chose to do so, it would be impossible. Unlike a commercial airliner, all the exit doors are remotely locked. To prevent accidents. Unintentional and otherwise."

"Unintentional and otherwise?" Molka said. "You must throw some real wild parties up here. But no worries, I don't have a death wish."

Sago's face brightened. "Ah, where there is life, there is hope. You do not accept your destiny too quickly, yes?"

"No. How about you?"

"The defiance of the condemned. Interesting." Sago turned to Maur. "However, she is correct, Maur. You are tired and not thinking clearly. Perhaps the injury to your head is affecting you.

Put away your pistol and take a rest. We are on the way home. Let us not allow fatigue to incite an unfortunate incident now."

"Yes, sir." Maur rose and left.

DING. The aircraft's intercom chime sounded, and a speaker voice said, "Pardon me, Mr. Sago?"

Sago pushed a button on his desk. "Yes, captain?"

"Sir, you asked for our ETA in Budapest. Right now, we place that at 10:06AM local time."

"Thank you, captain." Sago switched off the intercom and opened the back of the clock ticking away on his desk. He stopped the ticking, reset the time, restarted the ticking, closed the back, and looked at Molka. "Many people may find the audible machinations of this old clock quite irritating."

"You think?" Molka said. "I was about to throw it out a window. After I shoved it down your throat."

"All my wives would agree with you, on both counts. However, I do not find the ticking annoying. This clock once sat on the desk of Emperor Franz Joseph I. It ticked through some of the most momentous events and crucial decisions of 19th Century Europe and still survives. I take comfort in this when I must make a difficult decision myself."

"Are we going on that tour, or do I have to listen to your boring profound thoughts from now until 10:06AM local Budapest time?"

Sago smiled. "We shall begin the tour shortly. First, allow me to attempt to read *your* profound thoughts."

"Alright."

"As soon as we go aft, you will break my neck. You will next go bash Maur's brains in while he sleeps, wait for the aircraft to land, fight your way out, and make your getaway in Budapest. How close am I?"

Molka nodded. "Nearly dead center. Except after the aircraft lands, and before I fight my way out, I'll feed your dog's first."

"I expected no less. However, I will tell you why this will not happen. The very future of your people hangs by the threads of information I hold here." He put a finger to his temple. "And despite what your former masters may have told you, you will not be the last one they send to obtain this information. You now realize this too and will not again allow personal selfishness to

176

imperil the lives of others. Therefore, you are doomed by your virtues, and I am saved by my sins. Do you not agree?"

"I agree. Then again…." Molka smiled. "Nothing is decided until it's decided."

The tour commenced. Sago showed Molka the dining area set to seat ten, the lounge area with an 80-inch screen, the well-appointed galley, the guest stateroom occupied by a napping Maur, and his own Master Stateroom and bath featuring a king-size bed and a tub and shower with real gold fixtures.

The tour ended at the aircraft rear. Sago opened a plain door, and they entered a smaller compartment. Wrestling mats covered the floor. Mirrors encased the ceiling and three walls. Mounted on the fourth wall was a wooden BDSM cross and various restraints and bondage equipment.

Sago said, "This was originally a crew cabin. I had it reconfigured for Maur's recreational needs. I call this Maur's Playroom. What do you think of it?"

Molka smirked. "Maur's Playroom. Looks like wholesome fun for the entire family."

"Interesting you said family. On a business trip through the Pacific Rim, Maur once entertained a pair of sisters in here for six days and five nights. The screaming became intolerable though. It frightened my children nearly to ruin. I had the walls soundproofed after that. Now he is free to indulge as he pleases."

"Psychopathic, sadistic, *and* perverted. Maur's quite the exemplary employee, isn't he?"

Sago held up a finger. "As a matter of fact, yes. I obtained Maur's services, not in spite of his perversions, rather because of them. Perversions can be highly useful tools when trying to persuade a reluctant participant to close a deal."

"I wonder who's more perverted? The perverted man, or the man who uses the perverted man's perversions to do their perverted dirty work?"

Sago's face hardened. "Beautiful one, considering your present situation you should not presume to—"

DING. The intercom chime sounded again. "Pardon me, Mr. Sago?"

Sago clicked on an intercom speaker on the bulkhead. "Yes, captain."

"Sir, we have a possible issue with the FMS."

"I have asked you to use layman's terms when explaining these things to me. Do I expect you to know the finer points of exotic derivatives?"

"No, sir."

"What then, is the FMS?"

"I'm sorry, sir. The FMS would be the flight management system."

"What is this issue, and how serious is it?"

"I don't think it's too serious, sir. Most likely, um, incorrect data entered into the computer. I'm working on that now. But as a precaution, I recommend we land in Bermuda and have the equipment checked."

Sago sighed. "If we must."

"Yes, sir. Also, as a precaution, I've taken over manual control of the aircraft."

"And will that be a problem as well? You are a pilot after all. Pilots can still actually fly these days, can they not? I certainly pay you well enough to fly."

"Yes, sir. I mean, no sir, there's no problem with that, sir. There's something else, sir. The first officer is currently, um, indisposed."

Sago sighed again. "Indisposed in what way?"

"He's not feeling well, sir. He's in the lavatory. He's been in there since right after takeoff."

"What is wrong with him?"

"He, um, dined extremely native last night. What I mean sir, I think it's, um, a gastrointestinal issue."

"The imbecile."

"Yes, sir. I've been informed by Maur that our passenger is also a pilot?"

"She was a helicopter pilot in the military some years ago. Why do you ask?"

"Yes sir. Perhaps she could come to the flight deck and monitor the weather radar until the first officer is ready to resume his duties? Again, as a safety precaution. There's some significant storm activity coming into Bermuda."

Sago looked at Molka. "I think that would be an excellent idea, captain. Her company has become tiresome. I will send her to you immediately."

"Thank you, sir."

Sago clicked off. "You may go assist the captain now."

"Not unless I'm getting flight pay. This girl doesn't fly for free."

"You can go assist the captain or go back into the straitjacket and tell your jokes in private to Maur."

Molka smiled. "I know my way to the flight deck."

She barefooted forward to the first-class sleeping area, opened the cherrywood door at the front, and stepped into a connecting compartment leading to the flight deck. To her left was the forward exit. Sago had told the truth. The door had no manual release handle. What previous escape attempt horrors had necessitated that option?

Molka knocked on the flight deck door. The door was opened by a man wearing a white pilot shirt with black tie and first officer stripes—a tall handsome man: Warren.

Occupying the pilot's seat, a woman wearing a white pilot shirt with black tie and captain stripes—an attractive blond woman: Nadia.

Nadia peered over her shoulder at Molka. "Welcome aboard. Thanks for flying Air Langley."

CHAPTER THIRTY-TWO

"I'm either dead, dreaming, in hell, or in heaven," Molka said. "All better places than where I was before walking in this door. I guess what are you two doing here, is what I'm supposed to say. But what I want to say is, you guys know how to fly too?"

"She does," Warren said. "Former Air Force. Flew KC-10 tankers in the Gulf."

"That was a truck," Nadia said. "This thing is a luxury sedan. I mean, look at the size of this cockpit. It's roomier than our hotel room. Still getting used to the sidestick control though. But I can handle her, no problem. Ok, she's all yours, captain."

Nadia vacated the pilot's seat and stood next to Warren. The real captain vacated the first officer's seat and moved over to his rightful position.

Molka said, "And can I assume we're not on the way to Budapest?"

"You can," Nadia said.

"Alright, then what *are* you two doing here?"

"Returning a favor to an old friend," Warren said.

Nadia said, "Her happily relieved, confused face is freaking me out. Start briefing her."

"Certainly," Warren said. "Here's how this exercise was supposed to work. Your people recruited an asset who did a lot of business with Sago in the past—a well-connected entrepreneur out of Nevada by the name of...." Warren turned to Nadia. "What's his name again, partner?"

"O'Donnell."

The name hit Molka like another Taser shock.

O'Donnell was one of ours? Unbelievable!

Warren went on, "They tasked this O'Donnell with convincing Sago to crawl out of his hiding hole and come to the US for a very profitable deal. Sago agreed, and your people requested we detain him for their pick up. Easy, right?"

"Wrong," Nadia said. "Because the Corporation is trying to make nice with Sago's good friend, the Strongman of the East. At least this month anyway. So, in order not to piss off the Strongman, nothing bad could happen to his old pal Sago while on US soil."

"And once again, plausible deniability reigns supreme," Molka said.

"You've got that right," Warren said. "Request denied. And when you showed up, like we told you, it was only for Honey Pot intel gathering. Or so we thought. Until you hit Sago with your Indian casino snatch op. Horrible idea, by the way."

"I kind of liked it," Nadia said. "But it failed. You're in jail. And Sago gets to leave on time. It's over."

Warren looked at Nadia. "We even took today off."

"Don't start, Warren. Anyway, a few hours ago, we get an alert. You mysteriously got out of jail, neutralized our surveillance, have a biker army at your disposal, and are in hot pursuit of Sago."

Warren smiled. "When I heard that, I was almost rooting for you, Molka."

"Sorry I let you down, handsome."

Nadia glared. "You know, not getting rid of Maur right away was your mistake the whole time."

"I regret that too. But is this briefing rambling toward a point?"

"The point is," Nadia said, "it all never really mattered anyway. Because when you failed the exercise—"

"Be nice," Warren said.

Nadia went on, "*If* you failed the exercise, Sago was just going to be the victim of another unexplained disappearance in the Bermuda Triangle."

Warren smiled again. "A classic Azzur touch. The Strongman of the East is obsessed with paranormal-UFO-conspiracy stuff. This will drive him crazy for life."

Nadia said, "Your people are waiting for us at the Bermuda airport to take delivery of Sago."

"Azzur?" Molka said. "Wait. Stop the briefing. You just said Azzur. You know Azzur?"

"Yes," Warren said. "He's the old friend we're returning the favor to."

"You know Azzur? The same Azzur I know?"

"He's helped us out a few times over the years," Nadia said. "He contacted us today and told us about the exercise. He also told us he was the one who leaked your presence to the Corporation in the first place. Said he wanted to make the exercise extremely difficult, if not impossible, for you. Then he asked us to do this favor for him when—I mean if—you failed."

"But you got close twice," Warren said. "If not for a couple of bad breaks, you actually might have passed the exercise."

Molka laughed. "You guys keep saying exercise. Next, you'll tell me my task...this whole thing...was just a training exercise."

Nadia and Warren's faces became stoic.

Molka laughed again. "You better not tell me this was just a training exercise."

Nadia and Warren's faces remained stoic.

Molka stopped laughing. "This *was* just a training exercise?"

Warren grimaced, sympathetic. "Afraid so."

Molka punched the bulkhead next to her. "AZZUR! YOU BASTARD!"

"Don't take it too hard," Nadia said. "Azzur felt you needed a practice exercise before you'd be ready for the tough ones."

"The tough ones?" Molka said. "This one wasn't a tough one? Everything I did! Everything that happened! Everything I had to...it was all just an exercise?"

182

"This isn't a complete loss," Warren said. "Because Azzur also told us you'll still get full credit for your efforts. And it seems he thinks highly of you. And we think highly of you too. Right, Nadia?"

"Well, they probably think highly of you more than I do. But you've got guts and drive. I'll give you that. Work on getting the brains part under control and you might make it yet."

Molka dropped into the first officer's seat and looked down at the Atlantic. The setting sun toasted it orange. "Your old friend Azzur played all of us. Didn't he?"

Nadia shrugged. "Might want to get used to things like that."

"Speaking of friends," Warren said. "Some friends of ours in the lawn service business checked on your friend in the hospital. He's out of surgery. It's 50-50 right now."

Molka touched the Teuila flower hanging from her necklace. Loto said it brought good luck.

Good luck, brave Loto.

Molka pointed at the captain. "He a friend of yours too?"

"Not at first," Nadia said. "But he's decided to become friendly because he doesn't want to retire to the same place as this aircraft."

"Where would that be?"

"Classified. But there's a wild legend started by an episode of an old TV show that the Corporation owns this speck of an island near the Azores. It's not on any map, but it has a world class runway, a deep-water harbor, and an amazing aircraft and maritime museum that will never be open to the public."

"I watched that series when I was a kid," Molka said. "Overrated. And where's the first officer?"

"Probably waking up in the pilot's lounge back at the airport with what he thinks is the world's worst hangover," Warren said. "We dosed him."

"That just leaves the Maur problem," Molka said.

"Yes," Nadia said. "The Maur problem. Who told you?"

"Told me what?"

Warren looked at Nadia. "Her Maur problem is he shot her friend. Go ahead and tell her ours."

Nadia considered a moment and said, "A few years ago in Dubai, when Maur was bodyguarding another human piece of dog shit, he ran into a pair of female Corporation employees in a nightclub. They were non-combatants, just a couple of embassy technicians on a girl's night out. Two days later, their bodies washed up on the shores of the Persian Gulf. Both had been beaten and strangled. Before they died, each had an eye burned out and the letter M branded on one breast. He's been on our list since. But he's been lucky by being with all the wrong people at all the right times. His luck ran out today. We'll put him down before we land. We just haven't had time to figure out how we'll go about it yet."

"You won't have to," Molka said. "I'm going back there right now and kill him."

"No objections here," Warren said. "We'll even take out the garbage for you when you're done. And you can use this." He reached into a flight bag behind the first officer's seat, pulled out an FNX-45 semi-automatic pistol, and handed it to Molka. "He was nice enough to leave that for us."

Molka examined the weapon. "I like the man's taste. But I'm not a fan of gunplay in aircraft. I even talked Sago into making Maur stow his away."

"Nice work," Warren said.

Molka continued, "If I miss him, it could compromise the fuselage, or maybe damage a vital system inside it."

"Don't miss him," Nadia said.

Molka shook her head. "But with this beast, a hit might go right through him and do the same damage. No, it's too dangerous." She handed the pistol back to Warren. "I'll have to do it another way."

"Krav Maga?" Nadia said.

"Yes."

"Sure you can handle him with that?"

"I handled you without it."

"I don't think so, *ketzelah*."

"I think so, *kelba*. And I think you were ready to tap out."

"And I know you were saved by the bell."

Molka smiled. "Maybe we'll get a chance to finish that match someday."

Nadia smiled. "Look forward to it."

"We'll come with you, Molka," Warren said. "We'll bum rush him. He's a big bad boy, but he can't stand up to the three of us for long."

"You haven't seen his highlight video. But I'll do it myself."

"Don't be foolish," Nadia said. "We're all on the same team today."

"No, I mean I *must* do it myself." She stood and moved toward the door. "I'll be right back."

Warren blocked the door. "No way. Azzur's already steamed about O'Donnell. If we lose you too on our watch, we'll never hear the end of it."

"Why would he care about this O'Donnell?" Molka said.

"Your people have lost contact with him. They think we turned him, and Azzur's taking it especially personally because O'Donnell is one of his recruits."

Molka reached behind her head and tugged at the base of her ponytail.

This just keeps getting better!

"Please," Molka said. "Get out of my way and let me go kill Maur."

Warren put his hand on Molka's shoulder. "You have nothing to prove now. The exercise is over."

Molka pushed his hand off her. "It's not about the exercise! It's about...I don't expect you to understand...but in the mansion they caught me, interrogated me. What Maur did to me. What he wanted to do to me. What he said to me. What he made me feel. I have other things to do. Important things. Things I...things that.... I can't do them with this in my head. There's no more room. Either I kill him, or he's killed me. There's just no other way."

Warren shrugged. "You're right. I don't understand."

"I do," Nadia said."

"Then please brief me, partner."

Nadia moved past Molka and Warren and relaxed into the first officer's seat. "It's a woman thing, Warren. You wouldn't understand. Let her go. Good luck, Molka. Good luck on everything you have to do. I truly mean it."

CHAPTER THIRTY-THREE

"I take it the First Officer is feeling better?" Sago said when Molka re-entered the office compartment.

"He looks fine to me," Molka said. She joined the dogs on the couch. Sago still reigned behind his desk. Maur, fresh from his nap, sat in a chair across from her. She disrespected Maur with a sigh. "Don't you have other duties to attend to? Two dogs in here are enough."

Maur said, "She talks brave because she is scared, sir."

"You still think I'm scared of you? We stacked brigades of better men than you before morning chow."

"You mean in the IDF?" Maur laughed. "I say the IDF fights like women."

Molka smiled. "You're right. That's why we never lose."

"But you have lost now."

"Speaking of losing, how's your head?" Molka laughed. "You must feel like a *real* loser getting knocked out in your own house like that. I saw you laying there with your mouth wide open and drooling. The guys all posed for pictures with you." She laughed again. "I won't say what some of them did to you, but you...um...might want to go heavy on the mouthwash tonight."

Maur addressed Sago. "Sir, would you like me to take her to the forward compartment and put her back in restraints?"

Molka laughed anew. "Awww, now who's scared, little doggy? I've seen what you can do to a woman strapped to a waterboard, and with a gun at close range to an unarmed man, but how about a little face-to-face fun in your playroom?"

"The whore does have a death wish, sir."

"A wish we will not grant her," Sago said.

"Yes, sir."

Molka laughed again. "Yes, sir. Bark, bark, bark. No, sir. Bark, bark, bark. Thank you, sir. Bark, bark, bark. May I roll over and lick myself now, sir? Bark, bark, bark, bark, bark."

Maur burst to his feet, his fists clenched into veined iron balls at his side. "Please, sir. Just a few minutes."

Sago turned to Molka. "We have a long journey. Must you antagonize Maur?"

Molka smiled. "Yes, I must. And you're next."

"Very well, Maur. I suppose you have earned a little recreation. Do not maim her face. And do not burn her. You may cripple one small appendage within reason."

"Yes, sir. Thank you, sir." Maur pointed at Molka. "Come with me, whore."

Molka followed Maur aft. Enraging Maur was necessary to incite a fight, but perilous. However, her Krav Maga instructor had taught her that a physically superior opponent's rage can be used against them. Rage makes them prone to careless mistakes, giving you one vulnerable instant in which, you can defeat them. One vulnerable instant. It sounded reasonable. Then again, her instructor had never fought Maur.

Maur opened his playroom door and Molka stepped onto the mats in the mirrored square. He closed and locked the door, removed his shoes and socks, pulled off his shirt, and said, "In my country, in ancient times, wrestlers competed in the nude."

"Are we going to wrestle?" Molka said.

Maur dropped his pants and underwear. "No, we are not going to wrestle."

Molka raised her eyebrows in mock surprise. "Guess I didn't need to neuter you after all. Not much there to neuter."

"I give you two choices: a brutal raping followed by a moderate beating. Or a severe beating followed by a brutal raping."

"I noticed both my choices involve rape of a brutal kind."

"The only way I rape is of the brutal kind."

"Then my choice is death."

"Death is not an option I give you," Maur said.

"I wasn't talking about my death."

"Take off your clothes."

"What you did to me," Molka said, "and every other woman you've done this to, every other woman you've hurt, is here with us right now. I want you to take a moment and think of them."

Maur took a step toward her. "Take off your clothes."

"You feel them all here, don't you? Think of them. Think of me."

Maur took another step toward her. "Take off your clothes, whore."

Molka spread her arms. "Come do it yourself, little doggy."

Maur stepped to her, pressed his chest into her breasts, and looked down on her. "No. You will take them off for me, whore."

Molka drove a head-butt into his chin and fired a right-hand palm strike to his nose, breaking it, applied a neck clinch, pulled his head down, and twice kneed his exposed groin.

Maur pushed off her, stumbled back, and wiped blood from his nose. He then crouched into a wrestling stance, dove with shocking quickness into Molka's legs, and slammed her onto the mat.

Molka countered from her back with three hard kicks to his head, pushed off his head with her fourth kick, and got back on her feet into a fighting stance.

Maur dove for her legs again.

Molka side stepped and elbowed the back of his head.

Maur dropped, jumped up, growled, and came at her again high.

Molka swept his legs. He toppled. She caught his displaced nose with a fist strike and punished his lower back with an axe kick.

Maur rolled away, got to his feet, put his back to the mirror, wiped more blood from his face, and waited.

Molka got back into a fighting stance and waited.

Both took a cautious pause.

Molka strategized. She was winded. Maur was more winded. Her Krav Maga skills were unfamiliar to him. She needed to continue to use them to keep him off her, tire him out to even the odds some, then transition back to the attack. Convert any available items into weapons; she noticed a length of stainless-steel chain hanging on the BDSM rack. She had defeated many sparring opponents by attacking off the defense. But he was much stronger than the others. And this wasn't sparring.

Maur jumped suddenly over to the rack, ripped down the chain, and swung it at her head.

Molka ducked and side hopped. The chain missed.

Maur swung again.

Molka ducked and side hopped again, but not quick enough. The chain raked her cheek leaving a contusion and knocked her off balance.

Maur swung again. The chain coiled around her neck. He jerked with absurd force.

Molka forward face-smashed into the mats. He pounced on her back.

Molka twisted and sent a volley of elbows, forearms, and punches to his face. No effect. Rape adrenaline numbed him.

Maur cinched the chain on her neck, formed a noose, and in one violent motion, he stood and hoisted her into the air before him. He was hanging her, just like he hung the soldier in the sandpit video.

Molka clutched at the chain. It was too tight. Maur's dark eyes scorched her with endless hatred. She felt his mind changing. She wouldn't be raped and beaten. Or beaten and raped. She would be killed.

Over Maur's shoulder, she saw her reflection in the mirror, the last thing she would ever see. Her face exploded into crimson. It matched the pattern on her dress, which matched the flower pendant hanging from her necklace. Her lungs begged. Her life dimmed.

The necklace!

Molka's right hand grabbed the flower's bottom two leaves, pulled out the little dagger, and buried it into Maur's left eye.

Maur didn't scream right away. He dropped her to the mat.

Molka gasped hard.

Maur turned away from her, stepped close to the mirror, and puzzled at the blood flowing down his cheek and the oddity of the dagger handle where his eye should be.

That's when he SCREAMED.

Molka gasped more air and unwrapped the chain from her neck.

Maur screamed again.

Molka forced herself to stand.

Maur stopped screaming and restudied his reflected face in shocked confusion. He screamed again in confused shock.

One vulnerable instant.

Molka leapt at him, wrapped the chain around his neck from behind, and used it as a garotte.

Maur clawed her arms. Bloody hands slipped off.

Molka leaned back and pulled harder.

Maur clawed again and slipped again.

Molka leaned back with all her weight and pulled even harder. His flesh tore.

Maur descended to his knees. His arms hung useless.

Molka yelled for inspiration and pulled as hard as she could.

Maur sank onto his side. Semi-conscious. Dying.

No. Too easy.

Molka loosened the chain.

Maur gulped for air.

Molka dragged him by the chain closer to the wall mirror. Waited.

Maur gulped again.

Molka waited.

Maur gulped, coughed, and opened his working eye.

Molka ripped the blade from his ruined eye.

Maur screamed.

Molka pulled his head back so he could see his grotesque, wounded reflection. "That was for all the others!"

Maur screamed.

Molka skewered the blade into his healthy eye. "That's for Loto!"

Maur screamed.

190

Molka yanked the blade out and put it to Maur's neck. "And this is for me!"

Maur screamed. Not in pain. In terror. "NO! PLEASE, NO! NO! PLEASE!"

Two rapid slices. Carotid arteries opened. Blood spewed in majestic arcs and splashed and cascaded down the mirror.

Molka stood and watched Maur die.

But now you must learn my ways, Molka. Controlled violence—very useful. Uncontrolled violence—very dangerous.

"Go to hell, Azzur."

CHAPTER THIRTY-FOUR

Sago's face tightened from dreamy to dread when Molka returned from the playroom. Her once white floral-patterned dress was stained almost solid red.

"The tracks," Sago said. "Your feet. You have ruined my carpet. Have you also ruined...." He pushed a button on his desk intercom. "Maur? Maur? Maur answer. Maur, are you injured? Maur?"

Molka came to Sago's desk and raised the dagger's red-tainted blade. He pushed back in his chair. She moved between the desk and the chair and put the blade to his throat. Sago turned his head and closed his eyes. She lowered the blade and wiped blood onto his mauve shirt. He opened his eyes. Molka re-sheathed the dagger.

Sago kept his eyes on the necklace. "Ingenious. I...I take it Maur...shall not be...returning?"

"Not to this world," Molka said.

Sago looked toward Maur's playroom with pained eyes. "I never had a younger brother." He turned back to Molka. "My congratulations on your victory. However, it is only temporary. The first officer is also armed. I will ask him to join us."

"I was about to suggest that myself."

Sago pressed an intercom button again. "First officer! I am in danger! Come immediately with your weapon at the ready!"

The captain's speaker voice: "He's on his way, Mr. Sago."

Molka moved to the couch and sat with Sago's dogs. They leapt away and ran to their father.

Sago shook his head in disappointment at Molka. "I traded 72 virgins to Maur's former employer to obtain his services. Certified virgins mind you. Very costly. He will not be easily replaced. When I decide whom to trade you to, I will not forget this."

"Neither will I."

The compartment forward door opened, and Warren entered, pointing the FNX-45 at Sago.

"Meet your new first officer," Molka said. "This is Warren. Of the Langley family of Virginia."

Warren did a double take at Molka. "Jeez! You're a mess. Are you ok?"

"Yes. No. I don't know yet. Give me the weapon."

Warren handed her the pistol. "How's Maur?"

"He looks even worse than me."

Warren moved to Sago. "Stand up and turn around." Sago complied. Warren took two sets of flex cuffs from his pocket and cuffed Sago's hands behind him and his ankles together, then sat him back in his chair.

Warren turned to Molka. She contemplated the blood on her hands. She set the pistol beside her and rubbed her hands on her saturated dress. Warren stepped into the lavatory next to the office, emerged with a wet gold towel, and offered it to her.

Molka grated her hands on the towel. "In the Unit, on the missions, in the helicopter...my duties. I saw the wounded a few times."

"Molka," Warren said.

Molka continued to grate. "The after-action video. Infrared. Black and white. It was hard to tell. Hard to see. You know, the true horrible gore of it."

"Molka," Warren said again.

Molka looked up at Warren. "Is Loto going to make it?"

"You're fine now, Molka."

Molka scrutinized the soiled towel. "I'm fine now? Am I fine now?"

"Yes, Molka. You're perfectly fine now."

"Alright. I'm perfectly fine now." Molka wadded up the towel and tossed it at Sago. It landed at his feet. "And so ends the career of Mr. Gaszi Sago. The world's greatest businessman. The traitors' trader."

"May I ask you a question, beautiful one?" Sago said.

Molka thrust a fist at him. "Don't ever call me that again!"

"My apologies. Molka, may I ask you a question?"

"Leave her alone," Warren said.

"He's harmless now. Let him ask."

"Thank you," Sago said. "Molka, in your veterinary practice, do you believe in euthanization?"

"I believe in being merciful, if it ends cruel suffering."

Sago's face shouted dread. "Yes. Cruel suffering. I fear the fate which surely awaits me will be cruel. And I will suffer greatly."

"They're not going to execute you. At least not anytime soon. They'll get all the information they want first, then maybe dangle you as a bargaining chip to your killer friends. Maybe even trade you. Maybe not. Either way, you're going into a box. Indefinitely."

"Which some say can be an even more cruel and suffering fate than death."

"For me it would," Molka said.

"May I smoke a cigarette?" Sago said.

Molka nodded her approval. Warren took a brown cigarette from the gold box on Sago's desk, placed it between his lips, and lit it with a gold tipped wooden match from a holder next to the box.

Sago drew two lingering inhales and released two nose exhales, dipped his head to rest the cigarette in a crystal ashtray, raised his head, and turned to Molka. "If I may? For your consideration. Located under this desk is a panel. Under this panel is a large safe. Within this safe, US dollars, British pounds, Russian rubles, and gold bullion. The cash equivalent to approximately…36 million Israeli shekels. Your people, or his people," he nodded toward Warren, "will invariably find and confiscate these funds. Do you not agree?"

"I agree."

"You have shown yourself to be a cunning woman when you put your mind to it. So, spirit this wealth from this aircraft before they discover it."

Molka smiled. "You want me to have your money?"

"Yes. I do not believe I will have further use for it."

"True."

"Then why allow your overseers to have it? What would be a mere pittance to them would be life changing to you."

Molka smiled again. "But what about Warren, here? I'm sure he would feel compelled to make a report. He strikes me as a loyal corporate man."

"He is also an American. Simply bribe him. America is the richest country on earth. Therefore, Americans can conceptualize wealth like no other people. Which makes Americans the easiest people on earth to bribe." Sago looked at Warren. "Is this not the truth?"

Warren chuckled. "You're quite a piece of work, Sago."

"You see?" Sago said. "He does not even deny it. Think of it, Molka. All the worries of your life forever wiped away. All your wants and desires easily attainable. Think of all the good works you could do for the poor suffering animals of the world." His face lit up. "Think of living free with no one to answer to or for."

"Why don't you be quiet," Warren said. "You can't buy your way out this time. Can he, Molka?"

Molka leaned forward. "I'm still listening."

"He is correct," Sago said. "I recognize I cannot obtain my physical freedom. There is another way though. I offer you a fair trade. The combination to the safe, in exchange for one bullet in your gun. One bullet deposited into my brain."

"Sounds good to me," Molka said. "But how do you know after you give me the combination, I'll still give you the bullet?"

"Because I know, as you know, your honor will always be your burden."

Molka picked up the pistol, stood, walked to Sago's desk, and chambered a round.

"My children?" Sago said.

"Kept together and placed in a good home. You have my word."

"Thank you."

"Molka," Warren said. "Let's think about this."

"What's there to think about? He wants to die, and I want to kill him."

"But that's not what Azzur wants."

Molka shot Warren a laser-sharp look. "To hell with what Azzur wants! Where was Azzur when this snake's friend had me raped? Where was Azzur when this snake's dog tortured me and wanted to burn me and tried to hang me? Where was Azzur when this snake wanted to sell me to another snake? I don't care what Azzur wants! This is about what I want now!"

"No, this is bigger than you. Think about the consequences for your country."

"My country? My country. My country wasn't there for me either!" Molka turned back to Sago. "Will your family and friends miss you?"

"Yes. And I them."

"I have no family left. All dead. And no real friends left either."

Sago said, "The combination to the safe is—"

"Can you believe it? Someone my age having no family or real friends? Well, there's one person I hoped to make a real friend. But you had him shot. He's still alive by the way. No thanks to your dead dog back there."

"May I please give you the combination now?"

It would be easy. She gets the combination, he gets the bullet, and Azzur, the country, and the world get the finger. Probably couldn't spend 36 million shekels in 36 lifetimes. Might be fun to try though. Yes, give the world the finger and live for yourself for once.

But then what? But then what about my little Janetta?

"It is time, Molka," Sago said. "Simply pull the trigger. Take the money. Free yourself." The combination is 8 right, 12 left, 30—"

"I said shut your mouth, Sago!" Warren said.

Molka looked at Warren, then at Sago, then at the pistol in her hand; then she stared into silence. The only sounds were the muffled roar of jet engines and the sharp ticking of Sago's antique desk clock.

Tick.

Tick.

Tick.

Molka stepped close to Sago.

Tick.

Tick.

Tick.

Sago closed his eyes and smiled.

Tick.

Tick.

Tick.

Molka raised the pistol.

"Molka," Warren said, "you do this, and it will destroy you."

"Molka," Sago said, "you do this, and it will free you."

Tick.

Tick.

Tick.

Molka pressed the barrel into Sago's temple.

"He's not worth it, Molka," Warren said.

"You are worth it, Molka," Sago said.

Tick.

Tick.

Tick.

Molka cocked the hammer.

"No, Molka," Warren said.

"Yes, Molka," Sago said.

Tick.

Tick.

Tick.

"Time for you to say goodbye to us, Sago," Molka said.

Tick.

Tick.

Tick.

Tick.

"And time for you to say hello to the torturers." Molka lowered the pistol. "Maybe they'll accept your offer. I won't."

Sago opened watering eyes. "I beg you. Please, reconsider."

"You can't buy my mercy at any price. My mercy is my own, to give freely to the worthy. You are not worthy."

Molka handed the pistol back to Warren.

Warren exhaled into a grin. "I think you passed the exercise after all."

Molka knelt. Sago's dogs came wagging to her. "How long till we land in Bermuda?"

"About two hours," Warren said.

"Keep an eye on him, will you handsome? I'm going to go take a nap."

Molka entered the Master Stateroom compartment and closed and locked the door.

She entered the Master Bathroom.

Removed her blood-stained dress.

Started to take off Loto's necklace.

Left it on.

Stepped into the shower.

Washed the blood from her body and hair.

Stepped out of the shower.

Wrapped herself in a towel.

Found a brush on the vanity and combed out her hair.

Reentered the Master Stateroom.

Turned down the gold duvet on the king-sized bed.

Laid on the gold silk sheets.

Covered herself.

Closed her eyes.

And took the nap she had been chasing for eight days.

But before she did any of that, she sat on the edge of the bed, for thirty minutes, head bowed, fists clenched, weeping uncontrollably.

PROJECT MOLKA: TASK 2
TASK COMPLETED

CHAPTER THIRTY-FIVE

"You've never seen a guy as drunk as this little hillbilly," Loto said. "I mean he must have been walking around all day with a moonshine IV or something. Speaking of which, if you guys have anything a little stronger to juice mine up with, I'd appreciate it."

Molka, wearing post work-out leggings and her leather Vindicators vest over a hoodie, stood in Loto's hospital room doorway and listened to his story. His bedside audience: the Vindicators MC.

Two days previously, after landing in Bermuda, she had watched a new contractor team arrive in an airline catering truck, sedate Sago, put him in a large rolling food container, and drive him off to his fate. Nadia and Warren called a Corporation friend, who brought her new clothes and a plane ticket for her and Sago's dogs to return to Miami. Then they took off with the late Maur and flew Sago's aircraft into mystery, legend, and conspiracy. Molka last saw the captain very drunk and very confused in the airport lounge.

She spent the day after that eating comfort food, sleeping, binge watching TV, playing with the dogs, and nursing her wounds.

That morning, she received a nice message from an associate who said her car had been recovered, repaired, and dropped off in her apartment's parking lot. She then took the dogs to the animal hospital and left them with employees who assured her they would be kept together and found a good home. Next, she picked up Ramrod's bike, which was still parked at the airport, and dropped it at the Vindicators' clubhouse. The prospect on duty told her the Brothers would visit Loto in the afternoon. She would too. And say goodbye to the first person she had considered a friend in years.

Loto finished his story, "Anyways, this little hillbilly comes in the club and the first thing he does is take his shirt off. Why do hillbillies always take their shirts off everywhere they go? I told him to put it back on and he cussed me. So I bounced him. And what does he do when we get outside? He takes it out and starts peeing everywhere! Splashed my boots! I waited for him to finish. And then I explained to him that outrageous behavior caused by binge drinking is a warning sign of alcoholism. And he may want to consider getting himself some help."

"Then you just let him go?" Cuda said.

"No, then I yoked him up, dislocated his shoulder, and waited for the manager to call the paramedics. Damn-dumb ass hillbillies. But I shouldn't say that. I'm sure most hillbillies are fine people. And you know me; I try to love everyone. I'm just a humble man of peace."

"Yeah," Sparks said. "Baby's a man of peace, alright. When he gets done with you, there's a piece of you over here and a piece of you over there and a piece of you in the ambulance...."

The members laughed and were still laughing when Molka entered the room.

"MISS MOLKA!" Greetings came from all.

Molka went to Loto's side. "Whoa," Loto said. "That's a nasty mark on your cheek. And your neck's all bruised. What happened to you?"

"I'm perfectly fine now," Molka said. "How's our hero feeling?"

Loto forced a smile. "Thankful for the drugs. It hurts."

"Hell," Radical said, "it takes a lot more than a couple of 9mm slugs to kill a big Samoan mutha like Baby. His people eat handfuls of 'em for snacks."

"What happened to the big son of a bitch who shot him?" Yak said.

"Let's just say he won't cause anyone pain ever again," Molka said.

Bronco nodded. "Enough said."

"Your family settle things with that Sago guy?" Loto said.

"They're settling with him as we speak. Thanks to the assistance of the mighty Vindicators."

"Hey," Detroit said, "it's what we do. It's all about GEOD." He pointed at the GEOD patch on Cuda's vest.

"No one's told me what GEOD stands for," Molka said.

The members shouted in unison: "GET EVEN OR DIE!"

"I like it," Molka said. "And I may adopt it. What's the latest on Ramrod?"

"Caught a bullshit charge," Bronco said. "Judge granted him bail. Excessively high though. His reputation being what it is. The Brothers passed the hat. But we're still short. We're also passing the hat to help Baby with his hospital bills."

"I would like to contribute." Molka reached into her bag and handed Bronco her remaining task spending cash: a little over twenty-four thousand dollars. "Hope this will help."

"Yeah, that'll help a lot," Bronco said. "But, damn, Miss Molka. I mean…damn, are you sure? Because I'm not sure if we should take all this."

Molka smiled. "Don't think of it. It couldn't go to two better men."

"Thanks, Miss Molka! Come on Brothers. Let's go get the old man."

The members left. Molka sat in a chair next to the bed and pitied Loto. The ECG electrodes, the IV's, and his post-surgery trauma pallor presented a tragic sight. Yet he appeared almost angelic in the white hospital gown with his long black hair spread across the pillow.

"Thanks for coming," Loto said.

"I came to thank you."

"No, I still owe you everything."

"We're more than even now," Molka said.

"You're wearing my necklace. Bring you any luck yet?"

"You wouldn't believe what it did for me."

Loto smiled. "Can't wait for you to tell me all about it."

"Maybe I will. Someday. But I also came to say goodbye."

"You're leaving?"

"Yes. I expect my sweet Aunt Zillah will need me back home soon."

"That's what they all say to me." Loto struggled to sit up a little. "Molka, this might be the meds talking, but here goes. I know we just met a few days ago, and you said you're happily single and not looking for a man, and I'm probably not your type anyway. But if you ever were to look for a man again...would you even think about considering a guy like me?"

Molka smiled. "If I ever do seek a man again, I only hope he is half the man you are."

"Ha, ha, ha. I get it. Very funny. You're saying you're into skinny guys."

"No, that's not what I meant. I meant I only hope he is at least half the man you are in here." Molka laid her hand over Loto's heart. Then she rose, bent, and gently kissed him on the forehead.

Molka was approaching her car in the hospital parking lot when she received a message on her regular phone: the message she had been expecting all day. An associate informed her they had just dropped something off for her. It waited on a bench next to the fountain in the hospital's Healing Garden. She figured it would be a package containing her exit instructions. Procedures for how to inform the hospital of her unscheduled departure, where to leave her weapons in the apartment, time frame to vacate her apartment, where in the airport to drop off her car, flight home ticket info, etc.

She found the Healing Garden at the hospital rear. It was a secluded tree and flora-lined curved stone path. Soothing music from unseen speakers enhanced the ambience. She entered the garden and reflected on her second task.

She was lucky to be alive. She had committed enough reckless mistakes to get killed several times. Failed to complete the task too. Apparently by design, but it still wouldn't go over well with the Counsel. And killing one of their assets wouldn't go over well with them either.

But it was all so ridiculous, the plausible deniability, the deceit, the play acting. Fully grown adult countries behaving like little children. The nuances of global stratagems, as Azzur lectured her. Nuances. The road to failure is paved with nuances. She wished they would let her do things her way, the simple way—see target, destroy target. What was wrong with that?

Eight more tasks to accomplish. Eight more tasks, each promising to be more difficult. "The tough ones." Eight more tasks trying to break her. Eight more tasks trying to kill her. Eight more tasks to accomplish before getting the one she wanted.

Must get better. Much better.

Molka passed through an opening in a high hedgerow and stepped into a central courtyard. She spotted the gurgling fountain at the far end, but no package waited on the bench next to it—a man smoking a cigarette did. Azzur.

He wore a fashionable brown leather jacket and held a matching leather satchel.

Molka walked toward him.

I know what you're going to say.

Time for us to talk again.

Yes, it is, Azzur!

A training exercise?

Just a training exercise!

You bastard!

I'll never believe you again.

I'll never do another task for you.

You don't own me!

I can get rid of you.

I'll demand a new Project Manager.

I'll tell the Counsel what your man O'Donnell did to me.

Yes, I blame you for that!

Time for us to talk again?